FINDING HER MASTER

Crossed Wires, book 3

MARI CARR

LEXXIE COUPER

Finding Her Master

A forced-sex fantasy is one thing—waking to find a scruffy man binding you to a bed is quite another. Amy fights him, until she realizes her friend must have set up the sexy scenario. They've swapped lives, with Harper flying to Australia and lending her Chicago home to Amy. While she's surprised Harper would go to such lengths to help her fulfill a fantasy, Amy figures. . .why not?

After days of nonstop travel, Andrew arrives at the home he shares with his sister, Harper, with sleep on his mind—until he finds a naked intruder in his bed. Subduing the beauty, he assumes she's the blind date his pal had tried to set him up with. But would Mike actually sneak the woman into Andrew's house? Seems so. And he's not one to turn down such a gift.

By the time each has learned the other's identity, Amy and Andrew have shared the most intense sexual experience of their lives. And they certainly don't want to stop now.

Chapter One

Amelia Wesson—Amy to her friends—wandered around Harper Shaw's house in Chicago and resisted the urge to pinch herself…again. She was in America. She was really here.

For most of her life, she'd dreamed of traveling abroad, seeing foreign countries, experiencing different cultures.

Hazel Sullivan, the matriarch of Farpoint Creek Cattle Station in Australia, told Amy she had a case of wanderlust, and according to Hazel, she had it bad.

Her boss didn't have to tell her that. Amy's best friend, Josephine, had wallpapered every square inch of her room with pictures of Daniel Johns and Silverchair when they were growing up, but Amy had opted to display the photos of foreign places she'd torn out of old calendars. She'd spend hours looking at the pictures and imagining herself walking the city streets of New York or London, Rome or L.A.

And now she was here, in Chicago, in the United States of America. Yep. Definitely a pinch-worthy moment. Meeting Harper online had probably been the best stroke of luck Amy had ever had in a life full of nothing special.

Her mobile phone rang. *Speak of the devil,* she thought as she glanced at the screen.

"Hey. How you going?" Amy asked.

Harper chuckled. "You're going to have to start working on your American lingo, Amy, if you want to fit in. I'm *doing* just fine. Sitting in Sydney Airport waiting for the connecting flight to Cobar. Your friends better be there to pick me up so I can take over your life. Figure I've only got two weeks to completely wreck the impressionable minds of your students. I'm anxious to start."

Amy felt a twinge of homesickness as she thought about the life she'd so willingly traded away for this adventure. She was the teacher on Farpoint Creek Cattle Station, and her charges—children of the jackaroos and families who worked on the station—ranged from kindy to year six. Once her students entered their seventh year, they finished their education via School of the Air.

Thank God.

Amy's mastery of Algebra and the upper maths courses was shaky at best. Two plus two—no problem. Add in a bunch of wonky symbols and things took a bad turn.

"I've seen your lesson plans, mate, and I know you're a great teacher. I'm not worried about you messing up anything. Besides, the kids are so excited about meeting you and hearing all about their American pen pals first-hand, I don't think you'll have time to teach them much of anything. They have a list of questions as long as the Murray River."

Amy had come up with the idea of starting an international pen pal program a year ago and had gone searching on several educational blogs for an American teacher willing to join forces. Through some long, meandering series of clicks—she could get lost on the internet for days—she'd come across Harper Shaw, a fourth grade teacher who was also hoping to find pen pals for her students. They'd begun emailing, making quick introductions and exploring their ideas for the letter-writing lesson. Then the emails turned to IMs, in which they shared work war stories and lesson plans. Finally, about nine months ago, they'd started Skyping, chatting for hours each weekend about anything and everything. Though they'd never met face-to-face, Amy considered Harper one of her best friends.

"So what do you think of the house? You're there, right?" Harper asked.

"I got in about half an hour ago. It's gorgeous. You made a mistake offering this life swap. I'm squatting here permanently."

She heard a voice announce the departure of a flight to London through the phone. Amy could imagine exactly where Harper was sitting as she waited to begin the next leg of her journey. She'd be sitting in that same place in a couple weeks as she returned home.

Please don't let the fortnight go by too fast.

Harper scoffed. "The way I remember it, it was you who came up with this Freaky Friday idea of switching lives."

They'd been Skyping one Saturday morning in March —actually it had been a.m. in Oz, Friday night in Chicago—and Amy mentioned a movie she'd watched the night before. She couldn't recall the name of the film, but in it, two women had decided to swap houses, one woman traveling to America as the other took off for England. Amy had remarked that it was a great idea and probably the only way she'd ever be able to afford a big trip to America.

"I merely mentioned the movie. You were the one who said we should try it."

"I'm glad we did. Jesus. I can't believe I'm sitting in an airport in Australia. I'm bone-tired from seven hundred years on that international flight, but so freaking excited I feel like pinching myself."

She and Harper were destined to be friends for life. "I know the feeling, believe me. I've been so busy the past few days, getting everything settled at home, and then packing that I don't think it had time to sink in. Now that I'm standing here, it's just…bloody hell, it's incredible."

Amy had jumped at the chance to see Chicago, accepting Harper's unexpected offer before her friend could change her mind. For days they'd tried to find a time that would work best for both of them. They'd settled on Harper's spring break from work. Though the actual school holiday was only a week long, Harper had a week's worth of vacation days she was willing to tack on as well. Rather than push the trip off until summer—neither of them had wanted to wait that long—they'd booked flights for April.

"I guess you managed to find the key?" Harper asked.

"Yep. Right where you said you'd leave it. Under the third flowerpot from the left on the front porch. The house is so beautiful. I'm afraid this trade isn't exactly fair. I live in a tiny cottage twenty minutes from the station's main homestead. Nothing fancy."

Amy had rushed through every room of Harper's home when she'd first arrived. Harper and her brother, Andrew, had inherited the large house from their father upon his death nearly a decade earlier. While Andrew still kept a room there, the house primarily belonged to Harper.

As she and Harper spoke, Amy wandered upstairs once

more, thrilled to bits with the idea that this gorgeous place would be her home for two whole weeks.

She returned to Harper's bedroom at the top of the stairs. The classic décor and understated elegance reflected Harper's love of simple beauty. Her friend was lovely in an unassuming way. She didn't need makeup to enhance her natural healthy good looks. The room, though humble, echoed its owner.

The walls were mint green and that color was pulled out in the leaves of the soft floral doona covering Harper's queen-sized bed. There was a chaise lounge next to a bay window that looked out onto a well-kept garden bursting with flowers that screamed of spring. There was a dressing table with a chair and mirror—the sort of set Amy had always wanted when she was a young girl. The hardwood floor was covered with a soft off-white rug. Amy sucked in a deep breath and caught what she assumed was a whiff of Harper's perfume. The fresh, clean scent matched the room and the person who lived here.

Amy sank down on the bed. "I love your bedroom. It's so comfy and inviting."

"It's just a room. I cleaned the hell out of it right before I left. You're seeing it on a good day. Usually it's a disaster area."

"I did the same thing to my house. Scrubbed it from top to bottom. Of course, Thomo and Blue helped, so it wasn't too bad."

"Thomo and Blue?"

"Those are Keith and Marc's nicknames. You'll probably hear them called by those more than their given names. Listen, if you need anything, just find one of them. They've promised me they'll look after you. I reckon life on a cattle station is way different than what you experience in Chicago. Everyone at Farpoint is nice, but there are a couple blokes you want to look out for. Marc and Keith will make sure no one comes on too strong."

Amy had grown up on Farpoint Creek, and while there were plenty of women on the station, her closest friends were Marc and Keith. She grinned when she recalled the bon voyage party they'd thrown for her three nights ago. Amy rubbed her temple. She could still feel a bit of the hangover.

Her two mates knew what this trip meant to her. They'd even given her a going-away present—one hundred American dollars to spend on whatever the hell she wanted. Well, with one caveat. Marc had pulled her aside later to beg her to buy him a souvenir. As if she wouldn't. Her friendship with the two men was the only thing that made life on the cattle station bearable. Although she loved her home and her friends, she constantly longed to be somewhere—anywhere—else.

"I wish I could offer you the same protection, but I sort of purposely timed this vacation so that Andrew would be out of the country the whole time I'm away."

Amy shook her head. "I still can't believe you didn't tell your brother about your trip. Given his line of work, I'm sure he would have told you to go and have fun."

Andrew was host of a big cable show, *Off the Beaten Path* on the Travel Channel, and his job kept him constantly on the move. Amy continually pumped Harper for details about Andrew's adventures. The man was living her dream, traveling all over the world, exploring different customs, religions, foods, and she couldn't imagine a more spectacular life.

"You don't know Andrew. What's good for him is *not* good for his baby sister. He takes overprotectiveness to new extremes. If I'd told him what I was planning to do, he would have invited himself along to keep an eye on me. It's kind of hard to do something impulsive and spontaneous with your overbearing, older brother hovering."

"I'm sure he's not that bad."

Harper laughed. "Trust me, I'm painting him in the best possible light. He's actually a lot worse than that. As far as Andrew knows, I'm spending my spring break at an educational conference and I'll be too busy to call. Figure that'll buy me at least one week of vacation free and clear before he starts his daily checking-in routine. It's going to be tricky catching his calls the second week, what with the time change."

"You know, I think it's kind of sweet that he calls to talk to you every day." Amy was one of three girls, but she and her sisters argued more than coddled. Harper had become the sister of her heart, the one she reached out to in times of need.

"Yeah. Truth is I love him more than the White Sox, despite his caveman tactics. But even so, I'm glad for the respite."

"Well, I hate to break it to you, but you may have traded one bossy brother for two. Blue and Thomo can be just as domineering. They gave me an ear-bashing for days before I left about how I shouldn't do this or to be careful of that. We may not share the same blood, but those buggers have appointed themselves the role of my keepers. I'm afraid you might be facing more of the same."

"I'll keep that in mind. Crap, I took a Dramamine to keep from getting motion sickness on this next puddle jumper, but it's starting to make me drowsy. I hate flying in shoeboxes. Hope I didn't take it too early."

Amy looked at her watch. She'd adjusted the time as soon as she landed at O'Hare Airport. Mentally, she did the maths. Australia was fifteen hours ahead of Chicago. "It won't be long now. The connecting flight to Cobar is going to feel like an up and down one compared to the long-arse flight you just did. Keith and Marc will be there to get you. If I know Hazel, she probably pushed them out so bright and early it was still dark, just so they wouldn't make you wait. She's as excited to meet you as Thomo and Blue."

"I hope she likes me. It was really cool of her to let a stranger come to teach. No way that would happen in the States."

"Hazel will love you. Promise."

The Sullivan family owned Farpoint Creek. It was Hazel Sullivan who'd convinced Amy to go to Chicago and agreed to Harper taking over her position as teacher for two weeks. Hazel said letting her take the extended holiday was the least she could do, since it was probably her sons' fault that Amy was so unhappy on the station.

Dylan and Hunter had found American girlfriends in the past year. Actually, Dylan had married his artist, Monet, and was currently on his honeymoon. Monet and Hunter's girlfriend, Annie, had taken up residence on Farpoint and Amy spent countless hours talking to them about their lives in New York, as well as their travels to other amazing places.

"I guess I should get off here. It looks like they're about to start calling for passengers for this flight," Harper said. "Then I'm off to see your cowboys."

"They're not cowboys, Harper. Marc's a jackaroo, cause he's only in his early twenties and Keith is a stockman cause he's an old bastard of twenty-eight. You might want to brush up on your Aussie vocab too."

"Jackaroo, stockman. Got it. Oh hey. Before I forget, there are some staples in the fridge to keep you going until you get to the store—milk, eggs, stuff like that. The fresh towels are in the closet at the top of the stairs and the keys to my car, if you're brave enough to attempt driving in America, are on the hook by the foyer table. Just remember, we drive on the right side. You crazy fools drive on the wrong side."

"Bloody hell. I'm fine taking taxis or the train. Dying to try those things anyway. There's no way I'd risk my life trying to tackle your roads. I reckon I'd have a heart attack every time I had to make a right turn, fearing I'd smash into somebody. Those car keys will stay on the hook."

"Chicken shit. Fine. I planned a big surprise for you too. It's something you've always wanted."

Amy perked up. She loved pressies. "What is it?"

"If I tell you, it won't be a surprise."

"Where is it?"

Harper laughed. "It's not in the house…yet. So don't bother looking for it. And you won't know when it's arriving, but be ready. It'll knock your socks off! Promise."

"Crap. I hate surprises. Will you give me a hint at least?"

Harper refused. "Nope. Just remember to keep an open mind."

"What the hell does that mean?"

"You'll see." Harper yawned loudly. "Damn, they better start loading this plane soon or I'm likely to fall asleep in this chair."

"Okay. See you later, Harper."

"Bye, Amy."

Amy pressed End on her phone and sighed. If there was one part of the trip she regretted, it was that she wouldn't get to meet Harper face-to-face.

She wondered what the surprise could be. The two of them had shared so many secrets in the past few months, Amy couldn't even guess what Harper had planned for her.

A couple weeks ago they'd gotten drunk together via Skype, and Amy had told Harper things she'd never admitted to another living soul. Amy had been feeling sorry for herself for spending another weekend dateless and stuck at home, so she'd consumed a bottle of wine. On a whim, she'd drunk-Skyped Harper, surprised to find her friend also off her face.

Harper had been treating herself to early-morning birthday Bloody Marys, indulging in the same pity party. As usual, they'd turned to each other for company and spent nearly two hours laughing and sharing their dirtiest sex fantasies. Amy still blushed when she recalled the detail she'd gone into as she told Harper all about her sex-with-a-stranger dream. Of course, considering Harper's fantasy was to participate in a ménage, maybe they were even in the red-hot-fantasy category.

She glanced around Harper's room once more. She'd done it, found her way to America. Amy had spent hours on the internet planning her Chicago itinerary, making a list of everything she absolutely had to see before returning home.

She reached into her back pocket and pulled out her passport. Grinning at her foolishness, she lifted Harper's mattress and stashed it as Hazel's voice came back to her. "Don't leave that passport out in plain sight. Someone might steal it." Amy had asked who the blazes would want her passport, but Hazel told her to hide it just the same, so she didn't lose it. Truth be told that was probably her boss's biggest concern. She often lamented about Amy losing her head if it wasn't attached. So, for Hazel's sake, she'd keep her passport safe.

Rising from the bed, she continued exploring the upstairs rooms, walking farther down the hall and peeking into what appeared to be a catchall room. A treadmill covered with clothes sat next to boxes filled with Christmas ornaments, then there was a desk and a filing cabinet. Amy's own elliptical back in Farpoint served the same purpose—used less for workout and more as a clothesline.

She ventured on to the guest room where she'd left her luggage. Though Harper would be sleeping in Amy's bedroom—it was the only room available in her tiny cottage—Amy didn't feel right taking over her friend's space with such a warm and welcoming guest room down the hall. She stared at her open suitcase. She should unpack, but exhaustion was kicking in. Between layovers, flights and the taxi ride from O'Hare, she'd been traveling nonstop for nearly twenty-seven hours. Adrenaline could only take her so far. She was buggered.

She was about to collapse on the bed when a closed door at the end of the hallway caught her eye. She'd missed it on her first rushed tour of the house. Curiosity defeated tiredness.

The door was unlocked. Opening it, she stepped into the large room—and sucked in a deep breath.

The walls seemed to mimic her bedroom back home.

The stark white paint was covered with breathtaking color photos of some of the most beautiful places on earth. Several of the landscapes she recognized immediately from the pictures she'd torn out of travel magazines over the years. However, there were just as many places she'd never laid eyes on. The familiar ache in her chest returned as she realized how much of the world there really was to see.

This had to be Andrew's room. No doubt he'd taken the color shots himself, a photographic reminder of all the incredible places he'd journeyed to.

"Lucky bastard," she muttered jealously. The rest of the room was equally inviting. Andrew had a king-sized bed that looked soft as a cloud. Walking over, she ran her hand along the comforter, then the pillowcase. Silk sheets. Holy shit. She'd always wanted to sleep in a bed with silk sheets.

The room seemed less lived in than Harper's. The top of the dresser was devoid of knickknacks. The books on the shelf were organized a little too perfectly. Even the laundry basket in the corner was empty. If Amy didn't know Andrew lived here, she'd think this room was a second guest room. Of course, given the fact, the man traveled most of the year and kept an apartment in Los Angeles as well, it made sense that his room would look neater, less inhabited.

She considered returning to the guest room then changed her mind. According to Harper, Andrew was out of the country, spending the next three weeks on location in the South Pacific. Amy toed off her shoes then tugged off her blouse, jeans and panties. Stripping off her bra, she added it to the pile of clothes beside the bed and pulled down the sheets.

One night. She'd give herself one night between the silk sheets in the huge bed. Tomorrow, she'd move into the guest room.

Maybe.

***

ANDREW SHAW PULLED onto the road that led to the home he shared with his sister and released a long sigh. He was fucking wiped out. The last three days had been an experiment in torture when his shoot was cancelled due to a monsoon expected to hit the island he'd intended to be make number eight on his Best Kept Secrets show. He'd been in perpetual motion, hopping from boat to plane to boat and then another plane before his producer called to say they were scrapping the visit.

His phone rang, jerking him from his misery. "Fuck." One glance at the screen told him he wasn't going to enjoy this phone call.

"What?" Andrew said by way of greeting.

His best friend, Mike, chuckled. "Welcome home. Is it too soon to say I told you so?" Mike, a meteorologist, had been watching the progression of the storm and had told him not to bother getting on the plane in the first place.

"Yeah. It's too soon. Besides, you assholes are never right. How did you know I was back?"

"Tom called a few hours ago. Gave me the flight times. I just dropped Mars off at his house and now I'm headed home."

Mike served as dog sitter for his cameraman Tom's mutt. Given the amount of time Andrew and Tom were out of the country, it was probably safer to say he and Mike were co-owners of the gigantic dog. Not that either man seemed to mind sharing.

"From the sound of your voice, I assume it was a shitty trip."

Andrew switched on the windshield wipers and bit back a curse. All this rain was starting to piss him off. "It sucked. Did you call just to rub salt in the wound or did you want something?"

They had been friends too long for Mike to take offense at his sharp tone. "You on your way home?"

"Of course I am. Where else would I go?"

"Thought you might blow off some steam at the club. Wondered if you wanted company."

Andrew had considered heading to Velvet Chains as soon as he got off the plane at O'Hare. In the past, it wouldn't have even been a question. The private sex club was usually his and Tom's first stop after a long trip. It helped ground Andrew, relax him.

Mike had introduced him to the BDSM scene shortly after Andrew's twenty-first birthday. Mike's father and uncle co-owned Velvet Chains, so his friend had grown up around the lifestyle. Andrew had not. His first trip had been an eye-opening, life-altering experience. Mike jokingly insisted he'd known about Andrew's Dom tendencies since their freshmen year in high school, but he figured it was best to wait until Andrew was old enough to handle the news.

Lately, however, he'd found himself becoming bored with the action at the club. While the subs were quite pretty and more than eager to please, he struggled to find the same pleasure, the same sense of adventure he'd experienced in the early days.

"Thought you'd given up the club scene since settling down with Joanne. Married life already chafing, Mike?"

Andrew could imagine the goofy grin on his friend's face at hearing the name of his wife. Since getting married, Mike had adopted the annoying theory that Andrew needed to take a walk down the aisle too if he ever planned to be happy.

"I'd just be going for a drink. Joanne trusts me. Although knowing my sexy girl, she'd probably insist on coming with me."

Mike had met Joanne at Velvet Chains. There'd been no doubt the moment the two laid eyes on each other they were meant to be together. Though Andrew felt twinges of jealousy over his friend's newfound contentment, there was no way he'd admit it.

Andrew released a weary sigh. "I'm not going out tonight."

Mike was silent for just a moment. "Good."

Andrew felt his temper spike again. Mike had subjected him to too many lectures about his bachelor status, insisting it was time Andrew gave up his one-night stands with strangers and started looking for a serious girlfriend. Mike could be relentless when he got an idea in his head. As it was, he'd tried to set Andrew up no less than a dozen times the past few months with friends of Joanne's who would be "perfect for him". So far Andrew had refused every date.

"Don't start," Andrew warned, well aware of where the conversation was going. He'd rather hear what a fool he'd been to hop on a flight headed straight for a monsoon than be subjected to more haranguing about settling down.

"Hear me out. There's this friend of Joanne's we'd like you to meet."

Andrew gritted his teeth. "Mike—" he started.

"Before you start making excuses, I really think you should agree to a blind date with Amy. She's exactly your type. Pretty, submissive, sexy as sin. You'll love her."

"Not interested."

Mike released a long, slow breath.

If there was one thing Andrew and his friend were perfectly matched in, it was stubbornness.

"Fine." Mike's tone told Andrew he was far from finished, but at least his friend knew him well enough to leave it alone tonight. Even so, he wasn't sure Mike had ever relented so quickly. Andrew must sound more exhausted than he thought.

Andrew turned into his driveway and felt a sense of relief. He was home. His own bed was close. All he needed was to sleep twenty-four hours or so, and then he'd be back in fighting shape. "Listen. I'm home now. I'll call you tomorrow. Maybe we can get together this weekend and take in a White Sox game or something."

"Sounds good. Get some rest." Mike clicked off with a quick goodbye.

Andrew grabbed his suitcase from the trunk and tiredly walked to the front porch. The house was dark. Harper had left town shortly after he'd taken off for his ill-fated trip, attending some sort of teachers' conference in Minneapolis over spring break. He hoped her mini-vacation was fairing better than his had. He couldn't imagine anyone wanting to spend their time off doing what was the equivalent of more work, but Harper was nothing if not a devoted teacher. He felt the same sense of pride that filled him whenever he thought of his baby sister. She was the only family he had left in the world and he adored her.

Locking the door behind him, he climbed the stairs in the quiet house, not bothering to turn on a light. He'd grown up in this place, knew it by heart. He treaded lightly on the third step to avoid the creak, even though he knew he was the only one home. Some habits were so tightly engrained they never left.

He glanced through the open door to Harper's bedroom as he passed, the room bright with moonlight. As expected, her bed was empty. He paused briefly, missing her. She seldom went anywhere, so when she wasn't home, he felt her absence deeply. It was going to be a lonely week here without her bubbly, energetic presence. He'd considered going on to L.A. to stay in his own apartment, but he'd felt the urge to spend some time in his hometown.

Continuing down the hallway, he didn't stop until he reached his own room. The second he crossed the threshold, the hair on the back of his neck stood up.

Something wasn't right.

He quietly placed his luggage on the floor, forcing his eyes to adjust to the darkness. The curtains in Harper's room had been open, but his were drawn. The lack of moonlight left him blind.

Taking a few cautious steps into the room, he made his way to the window. Someone was here. He could feel it. Reaching toward the wall, he found his baseball bat. He'd played third base on his high school team, but he'd hung up his mitt shortly after heading to college. However, he'd never gotten rid of the bat, the hard wood now serving as the weapon he'd kept in the corner of his room for years.

Once he wrapped his hand around the bat, he drew it up, ready to swing. There wasn't any movement in the room, but he could definitely hear someone breathing near the bed. Approaching slowly, he almost tripped over something on the floor. As his gaze adjusted to the dark, he noticed the pile of clothing at his feet, then he managed to make out a lump in his bed.

What the hell?

Someone was in his bed, and given their deep, relaxed breathing, they were sound asleep. Turning back to the window, he quietly parted the curtains, anxious for some light. The person never stirred. Andrew kept the bat raised as he retuned to the bed.

With the moonlight shining in, he could see much clearer—and was shocked at the image of a naked woman in his bed.

He glanced around to confirm they were alone. The rest of his room looked normal, nothing touched or disturbed. The only thing out of place was the beauty who'd taken up residence between his silk sheets.

Andrew stood for several moments trying to figure out his next move. The rest of the house was quiet, but part of him wondered if the woman was here as a ruse, a distraction. Shit. He needed to lighten up on the murder-mystery books. He'd read two stories in the past three days as he killed time waiting in airports because of delayed flights.

He wasn't even supposed to be here. The only people who knew he was in Chicago were Mike and Tom.

The woman rolled from her side to her back, treating him to an unhindered view of her left breast as the sheet drifted lower.

His cock responded, stealing much-needed blood from his brain.

This woman had broken into his home. Somehow she'd known the house was empty. He fought down his arousal and decided to take action, to get some answers. He carefully put the bat down, leaning it against the night-stand in case he needed to grab it again quickly.

Then he slowly reached behind the headboard, silently searching for the straps he knew were there. He hadn't brought a woman back to the house in years out of respect for his sister, but he also hadn't bothered to remove the restraints he'd had installed when he was younger. Once the strap was freed from its hiding place, he walked to the other side of the bed, looking for the mate.

He took a deep breath, trying to calm down. He wasn't sure exactly what was causing the sudden racing of his heart—the anticipation of a fight or rock-hard, pulse-pounding arousal.

Moving ever so carefully, he reached for one of the woman's wrists, dragging it toward the first restraint. If he could fasten the straps before she woke, it would make his job of questioning her easier.

Unfortunately, luck was not on his side. The woman's eyes snapped open at his touch. She started to scream, so Andrew covered her mouth with his hand as she began to fight him in earnest. While he had to have her by almost a hundred pounds, the petite woman waged one hell of a battle. She scratched his face as he struggled to reclaim his grip on her hand. Despite her naked state, she kicked off the covers, freeing her legs to pummel his thighs with blows strong enough to leave bruises.

Forced to keep her mouth covered, lest she wake up the neighborhood with her screaming, he tried to subdue her one-handed. When that attempt failed, he released her mouth. The woman started to scream again, so he quickly grabbed her blouse from the floor and stuffed some of the material into her mouth, muffling her cries.

Her initial shock at being gagged gave him the precious seconds he needed to snap a restraint around one of her wrists. When she realized what he was doing, she doubled her efforts. With one of her hands out of play, it was easier to capture and restrain the second.

For the first time, desperation and fear crept onto her face.

"I'm not going to hurt you." His words sounded ridiculous even to himself. He'd gagged her and was now straddling her naked body, holding her legs to the mattress with his own after tying her to the bed. Regardless of who she was or why she was there, she'd be insane not to be afraid of his intentions.

She twisted her head, trying to dislodge the shirt from her mouth.

"If I take it out, do you promise not to scream?"

She blinked rapidly then nodded her assent.

He pulled the material away, ready to replace it if she broke her vow.

"Untie me."

"No." Andrew reached up to touch his tender cheek, his fingers finding the raised welts she'd put there with her long nails. "Who are you?"

Her breathing was labored, coming in hard pants after

their fight. Even so, her gaze hardened and he knew she wouldn't talk.

Something inside him cracked. He'd been traveling for days, stealing only a couple hours sleep here and there. This woman had broken into *his* house. She had some nerve acting like he was the villain. By God, he'd *make* her talk.

"I'll give you one more chance to answer my question. Tell me who you are or you won't like the consequences."

She stilled beneath him, her intelligent gaze sizing him up. He should climb off the bed and call the cops. If he was in his right mind, that's exactly what he'd do. Having her arrested would certainly be the kinder response. As it was, he wasn't in the mood to be merciful.

Instead of answering, she threw his question back at him. "Who are *you*?"

"None of your business. Give me your name. Now."

She bit her lip nervously. "I'm Amy."

Amy? Mike's Amy?

Andrew leaned back on his haunches, his mind whirling. Had Mike set this up? Past experience had obviously convinced his friend he'd never consent to a blind date. But would Mike actually go so far as to throw this woman into his bed?

Andrew knew the answer. It was more than possible. It was actually quite probable. Mike had the extra key to the house. He knew Harper was away and Andrew was back in town.

Andrew recalled a lifetime of little surprises his best friend had tossed his way. The high-class call girl who'd shown up at his door on his twenty-fifth birthday. The so-called conference that had really turned out to be an impromptu weekend trip to Vegas, complete with nonstop gambling and a private show with five of the hottest strippers Andrew had ever seen. Or this past year when Mike had managed to score tickets to the Super Bowl, but told Andrew they were headed to Indianapolis for his cousin's bachelor party. He'd let Andrew bitch for three hours in the car about missing the big game, only letting him in on the surprise when they'd reached the entrance to the stadium.

Mike was the master of the unexpected, so it wasn't farfetched that his friend would go to this extreme in a hookup. It would also explain his friend's easy capitulation when he refused to go on a date with the woman earlier. Mike didn't push the issue because he knew Amy was already here.

He grinned as his annoyance lifted. Amy was beautiful and feisty, with a hot accent. Australian, if he wasn't mistaken, though he'd need to hear her say more before he could be sure. His best friend knew he was a sucker for a girl with an accent. For the second time in one night, it looked like Mike was going to be able to say, "I told you so."

And since Mike had gone to so much trouble, far be it from Andrew to look a gift horse in the mouth.

Chapter Two

Amy frowned as the expression on the stranger's face morphed from anger to one of pure desire.

When she'd first woken up to discover the man in her room she'd struck out without a thought to the fact she was completely naked. Now, she was feeling far too exposed and vulnerable. If she couldn't figure a way out of this predicament, she was in trouble. Big trouble.

"I answered your question. Now answer mine. Who are you?"

The man no longer seemed quite as menacing as he had earlier. In fact, his eyes had softened, giving him an almost friendly look. "You know who I am. You and I have a mutual friend. One who's fond of surprises."

Amy blinked rapidly. Surprises? She recalled Harper's comments on the phone earlier. Harper had promised her a surprise, but this? What the hell was this?

The truth began to collapse in on her. It was her sexual fantasy.

Sex with a stranger.

Oh my God. There was no way Harper would set up such a thing. Was there?

Amy struggled to take a breath, her chest constricting with fear. She'd told Harper about her desire to be captured and taken by a stranger, but it was just something she dreamed about. Masturbated to while imagining the scene in her mind. Not something she ever intended to do.

You're in America, Amy. It's your time to go wild. Experience it all.

Of course, there was wild and then there was completely batshit.

Is it mental? What about the trip to a sex club you included on your Chicago itinerary?

She wished her inner voice would shut the hell up. She wanted to have a proper panic attack, not deal in common sense, however twisted.

"What are you planning to do?" She wasn't stupid. Maybe her love life had been stagnant lately, but she'd been around the block enough to recognize lust when she saw it.

"I think that's obvious, Amy."

She swallowed heavily as his gaze drifted lower, taking a leisurely tour of her body.

"You're very beautiful."

Reality tried to rear its ugly head, but she was running on empty. She was so tired, she felt numb…and receptive. It had been a long time since she'd been with a man. And she'd never, ever had sex with anyone remotely as gorgeous as this stranger. She had to hand it to Harper. She'd managed to set this surprise up when Amy's resistance was low. Her friend had also managed to find the hottest guy on the planet.

The man rose, leaving the bed, and for a foolish minute Amy thought he'd changed his mind.

She barely managed to refrain from demanding he return. Her mouth opened, then closed quickly. She'd gone crazy, lost her mind. A stranger had snuck into her room, chained her to the bed and now she was all but begging him to fuck her.

She cleared her throat, attempting to dislodge the lump that had formed there. "Where are you going?" She needed time to get her bearings, clear her mind and free herself from these straps.

The stranger studied her face. "I'm not leaving. I thought you might need a second to catch your breath."

At his suggestion, Amy sucked in some much needed air. Then the man sat down on the edge of the mattress. Amy's heart began to race. And not exactly in a bad way.

He smiled as he reached up to brush a stray tendril of hair away from her face. "We can slow down, but we're not stopping. You wouldn't be here if you didn't want this too."

She wanted to contradict him, explain that she was here to see Chicago, and that was it. But it was hard to deny his words when her body had begun to flush with arousal, her nipples going tight despite her better judgment. "This is going a little too fast for me." She tugged against the bonds once more. Maybe if she weren't so defenseless. "Would you untie me?"

He shook his head. "No. I love the way you look right now. Completely at my mercy. You know, breaking and entering is against the law. I should punish you."

There was something about the way he said the word *punish* that made Amy go completely wet. She squeezed her legs together and tried to ignore the tingles in her pussy.

"I didn't break in. I had a key."

His grin grew at her admission. "Then maybe I should reprimand you for fighting me." He touched the scratches she'd left on his face once more. She recalled the way his hard cock brushed against her hip as she struggled for her freedom. He'd enjoyed the rough play.

"You scared me. I wasn't expecting you."

He smiled, ran his fingers along her cheek in a way that was more friendly than sexual. "Yes, you were."

Harper *had* warned her. Told her to expect it. She just hadn't anticipated the surprise would be something so... so...shocking.

Exciting.

Harper had urged her to keep an open mind. Obviously her friend had known she'd balk. What sane woman wouldn't?

She studied the stranger's handsome face and her anxieties melted away. He had kind eyes and somehow she felt he wouldn't hurt her. Maybe she was being an idiot of epic proportions, but something about his face seemed almost familiar, though she knew she'd never met this man before in her life. The tension in her body loosened and she smiled.

"Beautiful," he whispered again. Leaning closer, he pressed his cheek against hers, his breath hot in her ear. "I won't hurt you, Amy. I promise. Just relax and let it happen. We've got all night."

Her eyes drifted closed when he kissed her. His lips traveled over her sensitive places, her ears, her neck, leaving no part untouched. As far as kisses went, her midnight stranger was a master.

He reached for her breasts as he continued to worship her face. He hadn't kissed her lips and she found herself wishing for a taste of him. It was as if he'd been pulled from her dirtiest daydreams and she felt helpless to resist.

"Kiss me." She hadn't intended to issue the request, but now that the words were out, she wasn't going to pretend she didn't want him.

He lifted his head "No. You're my captive. Tonight, I'm the one who'll be giving the commands. And you're going to obey me. Completely."

Her stomach flipped over. Jesus. Her stranger was playing the dominant card. She didn't consider herself submissive during the waking hours, but there was a part of her that had always longed to be dominated in bed. She struggled to remember if she'd admitted that desire to Harper. She didn't think so, but then again, she'd consumed a lot of wine prior to the sex conversation. Perhaps she'd told her friend more than she thought.

"Just don't expect me to start calling you Master," she said, purposely trying to tweak him. Test the waters.

He was silent for several breathless moments. "No. I won't be your Master, but you will call me whatever I tell you to, Amy."

It was a powerful assertion, spoken with absolute certainty. She briefly debated the wisdom in denying him then took the safer path. "What do you want me to call you?"

"For tonight, you'll simply refer to me as Sir."

"Sir," she whispered, trying it on for size. It was better than thinking of him as her stranger, but infinitely more dangerous to her libido.

"You know what a safe word is?"

Amy struggled to answer. Instead, she simply nodded.

His carefree smile faded. "I'm going to have sex with you. We can make it as easy or as heavy as you prefer. I can keep this encounter light, but…" He paused.

"But?" she prompted.

"I want more."

Amy tried to wrap her head around everything that was happening. She felt as though she was slogging through waist-deep mud in uncharted territory. "How much more?"

"Have you ever been tied up in bed?"

She shook her head. Only in her dreams.

Her answer surprised him. "Why not?"

Amy didn't reply. Didn't know how.

When the silence persisted, he prodded. "You like bondage. Your body is responding to it. I can see that. Why deny yourself something that turns you on?"

"I don't know. Where I'm from it's not that easy to meet blokes who want the same things I do."

He considered her words. "You're from Australia."

She smiled. "What gave me away?"

He laughed, the expression transforming his face into something that took her breath away. Bloody hell, she'd met her fair share of sexy jackaroos, but she'd never, *ever* met a man who affected her quite like this.

"Pick a safe word, Amy. We're going to play."

Her mind went completely blank. Once again, he filled the silence.

"Oz. Your safe word is Oz. Say it and we'll slow down, talk a bit, give you time to adjust. Fair enough?"

Was she seriously consenting to this? The man was a complete stranger. Sex was one thing, but he was offering a hell of a lot more than that. Just last week, she'd spent nearly two nights perusing websites of sex clubs in the Chicago area. She'd always wanted to visit one and experiment with some previously unexplored parts of her sexuality. What was so different about indulging in a night with this hot stranger versus one at a sex club?

About a million things—all of them having to do with your safety.

She closed her eyes and tried to force her weary brain to think, to overrule her wayward, reckless physical needs.

"Amy. Open your eyes."

She obeyed.

"Stop thinking so hard. You can trust me. I promise."

If Harper had handpicked this stranger to help Amy live out her fantasy, then yes, she believed she could trust him. "Okay. My safe word is Oz."

His smile grew, setting Amy's mind even more at ease. He reached up and released the restraints at her wrists.

She frowned. "What are you doing?"

He pulled her arms down to rest by her sides and she winced at the sharp pain. He didn't miss the look.

"I thought we'd give your arms a rest for a little while."

"Only for a little while?"

He gently massaged her tense shoulders, not bothering to acknowledge her question. If given his way, she had no doubt he'd bind her to the bed again before the night was out. However, he understood her reticence and was willing to give her a chance to accept that bondage without fear. She appreciated his kindness, his patience. Harper had outdone herself.

"We should establish some ground rules before we start. It's important that we understand each other's limits."

"You have limits?"

He snorted at her question. "I do. But I'd rather hear yours first. Is there anything you don't want to do tonight?"

She slowly sat up, wondering if he would try to stop her. He didn't. He watched with no reaction as she tugged the sheet over her bare body. Something told her this conversation was going to be unlike any she'd ever engaged in and she preferred to be covered.

"Is there a chance we could do this multiple-choice style? It's sort of hard to know how to answer considering I don't have a clue what you're considering."

He ran the backs of his fingers along the side of her neck, stopping when he found her pulse point. "I think that's a fair request. How about if I list possible scenarios and you simply say yes or no."

She nodded. "Okay. I can do that."

"Bondage."

She bit her lip, then let her body, her fantasies and her overactive imagination give the answer. "Yes."

"Spanking."

She sucked in a deep breath. "Yes."

"Flogger."

The air didn't reach her lungs despite her harsh gasp. "Um. Yes?"

He tilted his head, studying her face. "We'll revisit that one. Anal."

"Jesus. You just keep going for the jugular, don't you?"

He didn't reply, but his eyes crinkled, his laugh lines appearing.

"Okay. Yeah. We could try that…with a lot of lube."

"So noted. Nipple clamps."

She glanced around. "Do you really have all this stuff with you?"

"Don't worry about the details. Just answer the question."

Her nipples tightened, but Amy wasn't sure if the response was based on anticipation or fear. "Can we come back to that one too?"

His gaze narrowed, letting her know he preferred an answer. Unfortunately, she didn't have one to give. Suffering from a fuzzy head after two days of travel, she sort of wished her brain would tell her body this wasn't a good time. Problem was her body was all systems go and fucking horny.

He rattled off the next items on the list, one right after another with no pause. "Vibrator. Butt plug. Dildo."

"Yes. Yes. Yes. So long as they're new, not used."

He chuckled again. "Agreed. And not a problem."

"Wow. You're a regular sex shop."

His hands drifted to the sheet and he tugged it down. "Lay down, Amy."

So much for the get-to-know-you phase of the evening. She started to assume the position, but froze. "Wait. You didn't tell me *your* limits."

"I lied. I don't have any."

Bloody hell. She gave herself until count of ten to reconsider, silently saying the numbers in her head.

"Amy. I don't like to repeat myself."

His deep voice sent a sharp thrill through her. She hadn't mistaken her true desire for bondage and submission. She'd felt pulled to those types of erotic romance novels for years, devouring the delicious graphic details as she read page after page, book after book. Whenever she came across something she didn't understand, she'd head to the internet, her research almost always leading to daydreams that turned into wild fantasies that kept her vibrator busy, night after night.

Now here she was, a lonely Aussie schoolteacher, naked in bed with a domineering stranger who was promising to teach her some very naughty, very sexy lessons.

Who was she to refuse? For tonight, the teacher was going to be the student. Bring it on.

She lowered herself to the mattress, not bothering to reach for the sheet. The look in her handsome stranger's eyes told her it would be a waste of time.

Reaching for her hands, he lifted them to the pillow and placed them beside her head. It was a pose of surrender, but she didn't resist. She'd thrown up her white flag the moment she'd lain down.

"Leave them there."

"Okay."

He paused, obviously waiting for something.

"What's wrong?" she asked, looking around.

"When I give you an order, Amy, the proper response is 'Yes Sir'."

"Oh yeah. Right. Got it." She pasted on a look of innocence, knowing her reply would annoy him.

"You don't mess around, do you? Change of plans. Since you want to play the naughty girl, we'll start with a punishment."

As he spoke, he lifted her. She wasn't exactly a small woman. She liked her vegemite on toast as much as the next girl. Withholding that treat or counting calories wasn't something she was willing to do. Regardless of the extra pounds, her handsome Sir picked her up as if she were stuffed with feathers, putting her on her stomach with ease.

"Lift your ass."

"Excuse me?" She twisted her head to look at him over her shoulder.

"Wrong answer. Again." He gripped her hips none too gently, raising her. Then he forced her to bend her legs, resting her weight on her knees. The new position left her very exposed. And wet.

She didn't have time to consider what that meant before his hand struck her arse. It took her off-guard and it fucking hurt.

She started to rise, but he placed a strong hand between her shoulder blades and pushed her face against the pillow.

"Don't move."

"I'll bloody well do whatever I want," she said as his hand landed against her sensitive flesh once more.

"No. You won't," he said as he struck her twice more. She continued to struggle, but the man was strong as a horse. Amy's arse was sore from his spanking, however, she couldn't help but notice the heat was morphing into something infinitely less painful. She stopped resisting the blows. Her sudden capitulation caused him to cease striking her for just a moment. Then he picked up his rhythm again—his hand landing in different places along her buttocks and upper thighs. No slap was the same.

Amy started squirming again, but this time, she wasn't seeking escape. She was looking for relief.

He must have recognized her need. Gripping one knee, he pulled her legs apart then ran his fingers along her damp slit. She heard him release a long breath, a whispered "oh yeah" mingling with the air.

She gasped when he pressed two fingers inside her pussy. His actions were quick and forceful. After so many years with lovers who were too careful, too gentle, his rough claiming felt like a homecoming, only she was returning to a home she'd never seen.

"Harder," she begged.

He took her at her word, adding another finger, increasing his pace. Amy's fingers clenched the pillow beneath her head as she lifted her hips, shoving them against his delicious thrusts. He was fucking her into oblivion with no more than a spanking and his fingers. Bloody hell. Had she seriously considered refusing this gift?

Gray spots formed behind her closed eyelids. She was going to come. Her body stiffened in preparation, but he retreated seconds before she could close the deal.

"What the hell?" Impulse overrode common sense as Amy turned, ready to demand her due. "Don't stop."

His arms were folded. "Still trying to give the orders?"

"Fine," she shrugged, wishing her voice didn't sound so shaky. "I don't need you to get what I want."

After too many months of abstinence, she'd become an expert at finding her own pleasure. She reached for her pussy.

Strong hands grasped her wrists before she hit her target. "Wrong. You do."

Amy tried to free herself from his grip, but he was relentless. Within seconds, she was on her back, bound in the restraints once more. Her handsome stranger, still fully dressed, straddled her legs, completing the effect.

Why does it feel so good being trapped beneath him?

Because you're not exactly small and girly, but he makes you feel that way. That's why.

"Had your fun?" he asked.

"Not yet."

He grinned. "You're a shitty submissive."

"No, I'm not. You strike me as the type of man who works hard for what he wants. Where's the challenge if I just lay down?"

He tilted his head. "Christ." His brows creased. "You're right."

She lifted her eyebrows, surprised he'd admit such a thing. Marc and Keith told her she was too independent and outspoken for her own good. More than once, they'd referred to her as a pushy cow.

"I am?"

He nodded slowly. "Fight me all you want, Amy. Just be warned, I'll still win."

She yanked against his restraints, finding them too tight and definitely unbreakable. Yep. He was going to win.

But the best part? She was too.

He left the bed. Amy sucked in some much-needed air,

curious as to what he would do next. He'd painted some naughty pictures in her mind with his talk of nipple clamps and vibrators.

She glanced around the room wondering where he'd hidden his bag of tricks. Had he stowed it in the house prior to her arrival or carried it in with him tonight? Given the fact the restraints had already been attached to the bedframe, she suspected he'd set the scene earlier.

Reaching for the buttons on his shirt, he slowly slipped each one from its hole. He knew she'd been on the verge of an orgasm. He obviously intended to punish her for her outspokenness by leaving her in need.

Arsehole.

God, he's hot.

At some point, he'd parted the curtains. Thankfully, the full moon was providing plenty of light for his sexy strip-tease. Once he shrugged off his shirt, he started on the fastening to his pants.

No wonder he'd been able to pose her like a bloody Barbie doll. He was built. His arms were muscular and she'd take *his* six-pack over a half dozen ice-cold Toohey's Dry any day.

She licked her lips when he shoved his trousers down. Either he'd tugged the underwear off with the rough cotton or he went commando.

Either way, she didn't care.

Holy. Fuck.

The brief touches of his covered cock had teased her since she'd agreed to this adventure, but the too-quick rubs hadn't really clued her in to what he was hiding beneath his pants.

He didn't return to the bed immediately. Instead, he let her look her fill like a man who was perfectly comfortable in his own skin. She was no stranger to cocky, self-confident men. Australia seemed to raise that breed in abundance, Marc and Keith leading the pack.

Unfortunately, she'd never managed to attract that type back home.

No. Scratch that. Attraction wasn't part of it. Her list of dating prospects was lacking because Blue and Thomo had the annoying tendency of warning away men they didn't think worthy of her. That practice ticked her off most of the time, but she couldn't help noticing none of the men ever stuck around to fight for a date with her. And that pissed her off even more.

Something told her that her best mates wouldn't intimidate this man.

He reached for his hard, thick cock and slowly stroked it, his gaze never leaving hers. Her fingers itched for a touch and her mouth watered for a taste.

Bending forward, he dug around under the bed for something.

Ah, so that was where he'd stashed his bag of tricks.

Her mind whirled with curiosity, wondering what wonderful sexual torment he was plotting. She was disappointed when he came up with nothing more than a scarf.

"I'm already tied up. Doesn't that seem a bit redundant?"

He chuckled, but didn't respond. Instead, he lifted the silk to her eyes.

Oh shit.

Her heart had only just stopped racing. Now it kick-started back to life, pounding almost painfully as he tied the scarf in place. He knew his stuff. He'd managed to plunge her into complete darkness.

Losing the use of her hands had been equal parts frightening and titillating, however, losing her sight was downright terrifying. And exhilarating.

"What are you going to do?"

His hand touched her throat and she jerked at the unexpected caress.

"Shh," he soothed. "Calm down, Amy. I promised I wouldn't hurt you."

"Yeah right. And then you spanked my arse. It's still on fire, by the way."

Her words seemed to remind him of his earlier actions. His fingers drifted along her side, not stopping until they reached her hip.

When he spoke, his breath tickled her cheek. When had he leaned so close? "You like the fire and the pain. Those hurts don't count."

She wanted to ask him what qualified if that didn't, but deep inside, she already knew the answer. "Tell me your name." It bothered her that she didn't know. He'd told her to call him Sir, but she wanted more of him than that. Maybe the original fantasy had been sex with a stranger, but somewhere along the course of the evening, it had changed. Now she only wanted sex with him.

"You know my name."

She wanted to push the issue, but he was right. Harper had designed this night according to her desires. It would be wrong to change the game now.

"Fine. I want you to touch me." She hesitated for only a second before adding, "Sir."

"Very nice. I think that deserves a reward."

A reward sounded wonderful. Hell, given how hot her punishment had left her, she felt optimistic this was going to be good.

When his lips latched to her nipple, sucking gently, she sighed. She was right. This was very good. Soon, he increased the suction until she cried out. Then he turned his attention to her other nipple, repeating the process.

Amy squeezed her legs together, the pressure in her pussy building until it was almost painful. She'd been too close before. Her body hadn't forgotten, or forgiven him for pulling up short.

"Please," she whispered.

"Too soon. We haven't pushed any of those limits yet."

"I don't care. I need more."

He returned to her nipple, but this time it wasn't his lips that issued the sexy pain, it was his teeth. He nipped at her distended flesh as she groaned and tugged against the restraints. She suddenly missed the use of her hands. She wanted to press his lips and teeth against her breasts and force him to do her bidding. Then she'd push him lower, demanding he use that sexy mouth where it would do the most good.

Unfortunately, he'd left no doubt he was in control. He'd guide the play and, regardless of her wishes, she'd get what he gave her and no more.

Worst part was acknowledging it was *that fact* that was making her so freaking hot. She was powerless and reveling in it.

He left the bed and the sound that escaped her lips couldn't be called anything other than a whimper. Jesus. Who was she tonight?

"I'm coming right back."

Again, she heard rustling under the bed. As the mattress sank under his weight, his lips found their way to her breasts again. He certainly didn't believe in skimping on foreplay.

Her nipples were so hard, they could cut glass.

"This will pinch."

She started to ask what he meant, but before she could form the question, he put something on her right nipple.

She yelped at the unexpected pain. Pinch was an understatement.

"Bloody hell."

"It's a nipple clamp."

She considered adding the wicked clamp to her list of *Not Bloody Likely*, but—like the spanking—once the initial sting faded, the pain changed to something better. At least it did until he placed a clamp on her other nipple.

She released a pained moan, her eyelids scrunching beneath the blindfold. "God."

He didn't remove the clamps despite her comments, and she realized she hadn't said the safe word. He wouldn't acknowledge her complaints or cries until she uttered Oz. That realization was comforting. She wouldn't have to shield her initial reactions or pretend for fear he'd stop.

As the pain in the second nipple eased, his attention seemed to drift lower.

"Open your legs, Amy."

She'd pressed them together so tightly, she feared they'd cramp up. "I can't. Hurts. Horny."

Again, he ignored her protest. He gripped her knees and pulled them apart. "Leave them open or I'll tie your ankles to the bedposts as well."

There are more restraints on the bed?

She forced air in and out in an attempt to calm down. Her body was on system overload. At this point, he only need blow in her ear and she was in danger of going off like a frog in a sock.

The mattress shifted again under his weight. She felt him settle between her outstretched legs. She'd never considered herself a religious woman, but that didn't stop her from praising any and every higher being known to humans.

He nipped at her clit with those wicked teeth of his.

Amy squealed with surprise…and delight. When his tongue trailed along her slit, she knew she'd died and gone to heaven. God bless Chicago.

Her fantasy lover read her far too well and he used that knowledge against her. With his lips, tongue, teeth and fingers, he drove her to the edge of an orgasm, over and over again. Every time, he stopped just before she could find release.

"You bloody bastard," she screamed when he pulled away for the fifth time. Her wrists were sore from fighting against the restraints. She didn't want her freedom as much as she wanted to beat the hell out of him.

"Sweet talking will get you nowhere."

"Fuck me. Now. I mean it."

He chuckled. "Ask me nicely."

Sweat trickled from her brow along her hairline.

"You do realize I'm going to kill you the second you take these straps off my wrists."

Clearly he was undeterred. He gripped her breast and told her to hold her breath. She opened her mouth to ask why, but just then, he released the clamp.

She screamed as the sensation of needles piercing flesh assailed her. Tears formed in her eyes but the blindfold quickly absorbed the moisture.

He soothed the pain away with soft kisses, his tongue caressing the wounded tip. Her head was dazed, her body overwhelmed by his continual sensual assaults. She'd never realized pain, when paired with pleasure, could be such a heady aphrodisiac. She wanted more.

"Ready for the second?"

She nodded slowly, preparing herself for the onslaught. While the removal of the second clamp was just as painful, she was able to tolerate it better, her body anticipating its delicious reward. He didn't disappoint her as he eased the pain with his talented mouth.

Once the sweet agony passed, he removed the blindfold. She struggled to adjust to the bright moonlight. Then he unfastened the restraints around her wrists. She lowered her arms slowly, gaze never leaving his face as she tried to anticipate his next move.

Laugh lines formed around his eyes. "If you're still planning to kill me, do it now. Otherwise, roll over and lift your ass in the air again."

She didn't even feign annoyance. She was too far gone, putty in his hands. She twisted beneath him, anxious for more. She started when his hands touched her sore arse, expecting him to spank her for her threats.

Instead, he bent lower and placed a kiss on one of her buttocks. "Your ass is gorgeous."

She laughed until he pressed her legs apart and ran his hand along her slit once more. His fingers lingered around her anus and she bit her lip. That was uncharted territory for her, though it wasn't due to a lack of interest on her part. She'd had one somewhat serious boyfriend in her life, Kyle, and he'd considered "backdoor" activities disgusting.

Marc and Keith had laughed their arses off when she'd shared that tidbit with them one night after too many shots of Bundy. Then they'd told her to dump the uptight dickhead. She'd scoffed at their suggestion, but the next day, hungover from the rum, she'd followed their advice and broken things off. Since then, she'd lived a life more celibate than a nun's, wondering at least a million times a day if boring, vanilla sex with Kyle was preferable to no sex at all. She decided against Kyle every time.

Her sexy stranger wiggled his finger against her tight opening, bringing her thoughts back to the present. "You said yes as long as we use lots of lube."

When they'd discussed limits, she'd thought he was just jerking her chain a bit, trying to get a rise out of her and having some fun at her expense. Apparently not. So far, he'd made good on the spanking, the nipple clamps and the bondage. She wasn't sure how much more her over-wrought body could take.

"Um. Crap. Oz. Just for a second. Oz."

He leaned back on his haunches as she sat up to face him. His face was more understanding than she'd expected. Truthfully, she was afraid he'd be angry with her.

"Sorry," she said softly.

He grasped her hand. "Not a problem, Amy. I warned you before we started, you make me want more. I shouldn't have pushed you so hard."

"It's not that. Bloody hell. Tonight's ranking up there as my single greatest sexual experience and I haven't even come yet."

He laughed. "What's wrong with the men in Australia?"

"Nothing. I mean, they're okay blokes."

"I love your accent."

She shrugged. "It's alright."

He shifted, sitting as he tugged on her hand, dragging her closer until she was straddling his thighs. His erect cock rested tightly against the seam of her pussy.

Helllloooo, Mr. Wiggly.

She resisted the urge to giggle nervously. The nickname came from one of the more precocious tots amongst her year one kids, Nige. She'd lost count of how many times she'd put him in time-out for pulling out his own Mr. Wiggly and showing it to the girls.

She blushed again.

Wow. Really? You're sitting on the hardest, most amazing cock you've ever seen and you're thinking about work? Wonder why you're not getting laid on a regular basis, Amy?

"You okay?" He shifted slightly and his hard-on brushed against her clit.

"Oh yeah." Her quick, breathless response pleased him.

"Good." He pressed her back against the mattress, covering her with his body. He was big…everywhere. Kyle had been slight, only about an inch taller than her. Apart from him and a couple unmemorable one-night stands prior to him, it was safe to say she'd never been with such a large man. She liked it.

He reached toward the nightstand and she followed his progress, watching as he pulled a condom out of the drawer. Talk about prepared. Her sexy stranger had set up the room perfectly. She wondered what Andrew Shaw would think about the illicit activities taking place in his room.

Wait…

How did Harper know she would pick this room?

The thought caught her unaware and a seed of doubt sprouted in the back of Amy's mind.

Unfortunately, it didn't have time to take root, mainly because her stranger had decided to do a bit of rooting himself. Donning the condom, he placed the head of his cock at the opening of her pussy.

She had only a moment to regret halting his anal play. Her damn reticence had cost her a new experience. Maybe she'd talk him into trying again later.

After.

Because there was no way she was stopping him now. He pressed in slowly as Amy struggled to suck air into her lungs. Her eyes hadn't deceived her. He was definitely filling her in a way she'd never been filled before.

Once he was fully seated, he paused for the briefest of seconds. "Hold on."

It was the only warning she received as he unleashed the same incredible strength and power he'd exposed her to all night.

He pounded into her body, offering her no reprieve. Not that she wanted it. Amy lifted her legs, wrapping them around his waist, opening herself to him even more.

Both of them groaned as he thrust in deeper.

"So bloody good." She dragged her nails along his back. Two could play the pleasure-pain game. He hissed sharply, but his gaze told a different tale as it narrowed with hunger, his lust bared before her.

"Don't come," he warned her.

"What? Fuck that."

He drove in harder, then stalled. "I mean it, Amy. You're going to do what I say at least once tonight. I'll tell you when to come. Don't you dare do it a second before that."

He punctuated his demand with a thrust that cut too deep, too close to the hot zone.

"Not. Sure. I. Can. Stop." Each word was drawn from her on a harsh breath.

"Just a minute more, Amy. Just a minute and we'll come together."

His demand, combined with the slightest tinge of a plea, touched her. She closed her eyes. "Yes Sir."

"No. Fuck. I changed my mind. Call me Andrew. Say my name. Say it and come."

She exploded into a million pieces, her lips forming the word. "Andrew!" she cried. "God, Andrew. Andrew."

Tremors racked her frame, shaking her bones so strongly she feared she'd break. Had she ever had an orgasm before now? There was no way she could compare those lukewarm imposters to this climax.

Andrew followed her into oblivion, his arms tightening as he bucked, his cock jerking with its release.

"Jesus," he said breathlessly. He kissed her lightly, his lips lingering despite the fact both of them were gasping. It was the sweetest of kisses.

Finally, regretfully, he released her lips, lifted and moved out of her body. She pressed her legs together, wishing there was some way to hold on to the feeling of being filled by him forever.

From the corner of her eye, she saw him pull off the condom and toss it into the small trashcan beside the bed.

Then, as always, he used his undeniable strength to put Amy where he wanted. He twisted her boneless body to its side until he was spooning her. Their bodies curved together as if they were puzzle pieces, a perfect fit.

Amy and Andrew.

Andrew.

His name niggled at her sleepy, sex-overloaded brain, as did the restraints and the sex toys in the wrong room.

Andrew.

Amy's eyes flew open.

Mother of God, she'd just slept with Harper's brother!

She was naked and twisted up like a pretzel with Andrew Shaw.

The truth of what she'd done crashed down on her like atomic bombs from an attacking army. Tonight wasn't a setup, though it definitely qualified as a surprise. Andrew had come home early and, in her sleep-deprived state, she'd convinced herself Harper had hooked her up with a fantasy lover. Had that answer actually made sense to her at some point?

Fuckity-fuck-fuck.

She'd fucked up.

And she fucked her friend's brother.

Bloody hell. She was *so* fucked.

And while she knew now she'd made a whopper of a mistake, one question still remained.

Who the fuck did he think *she* was?

Chapter Three

Andrew rose much earlier than he expected the morning after his incredible night with Amy. He studied the tired face of his midnight visitor. She slept the sleep of the dead. He didn't blame her. If he weren't so jet-lagged, and if his internal clock wasn't so screwed up, he'd probably still be down for the count as well.

Rising, he crossed to his dresser and dug around for a pair of sweatpants. Throwing them on, he walked to the bathroom to brush his teeth and shave. His thick beard grew in quickly and it had been at least four days since his face had seen a razor thanks to the trip from hell. His onscreen persona was always clean-shaven, so he wasn't used to the scruffy man in the mirror.

He grimaced at his reflection. The circles under his eyes were too dark, his face lined with tiredness. He saw a nap in his very near future. It would probably take him a day or two to get his system sorted out.

One thing he'd never managed to overcome with his job was the adjustments to the ever-changing time zones. No matter how many cross-country journeys he made, he still suffered a sort of day-after hangover, struggling for twenty-four hours to adapt to the new time.

For a moment he considered calling Mike, but dismissed the idea. There was no way he was giving his cocky friend yet another opportunity to rub Andrew's nose in something. Actually, it would serve Mike right if Andrew simply avoided his calls for a few days. His best friend was as meddlesome as a tabloid reporter. It might be fun to make Mike suffer for a while, wondering how his night with Amy turned out.

Amy. His mind whirled over everything that had happened last night. She'd pulled him out of his misery, giving him some of the best sex of his life. He wasn't sure what made her different from the women he usually hooked up with at Velvet Chains. Perhaps it was just as she'd said. She didn't submit easily. He typically played with the same subs at the club. They were well-trained, obedient. Boring. He missed the challenge.

Amy had pushed him out of his all-powerful Dom role and forced him to work for his reward. She wasn't passive. Instead, she was refreshing, fun. Mike would have a field day with that knowledge.

Despite her obvious inexperience, he hadn't pulled any punches, hadn't handled her with kid gloves. And she'd taken to his rough touches like a rock star to the spotlight.

He returned to the bedroom. Picking up his phone from the nightstand, he took one last look at the bed. His midnight visitor was even prettier in daylight.

He rolled his eyes. Christ. He was acting like a smitten teenager with his first girlfriend.

Get a grip, Shaw.

It was just sex. Incredible, blow-your-balls-off sex. But *just sex* nonetheless.

Amy showed no signs of rising soon, so he headed for

the kitchen. He needed coffee to clear his head. The bright light of morning and the few hours of sleep he'd managed to snag were bringing too much clarity to his not-quite-as-tired mind. Something was wrong, but he couldn't figure out what.

Heading down the hallway, he glanced in the guest room as he passed—

He paused.

There was an unfamiliar suitcase resting open on the bed. Amy's? Had she been so certain of her success with him that she'd packed a bag?

The idea bothered him. Entering the room, he casually looked to see what she'd brought with her. The clothing didn't look like the stuff a woman would use to seduce a man. No sexy lingerie or revealing outfits. In fact, with the exception of one pretty hot leather miniskirt, there was nothing more than jeans and regular tops, a bathroom bag and a travel book about Chicago.

What the hell? It appeared Amy had come here straight from the airport. Maybe he'd place a call to Mike after all. Somehow the pieces to this puzzle weren't fitting together. Time to ask some questions.

Andrew continued to the kitchen, filled the coffeepot with water and counted out twelve scoops. He added another for good measure. Something told him he needed a strong brew today. A quick glance at the clock confirmed it was almost nine. Not too early to call his friend.

He picked up his phone and dialed. Mike answered with a chipper "hello". Idiot man had always been a morning person.

"Hey, Mike. What's Amy look like?"

"What?"

Andrew sighed. "The girl you want to fix me up with. What does she look like?"

There was a slight pause on the other end. "Never known you to be so shallow, Andrew. Why does it matter?"

"It doesn't. I'm just curious. Describe her."

Mike started rattling off a list of physical attributes that basically told him nothing. "Brown hair, brown eyes, nice figure, medium height."

The adjectives were too bland for Amy's chestnut tresses, chocolate-brown eyes and curves, but they still fit. "Does she have an accent?"

"What the hell kind of question is that?"

Andrew gritted his teeth. "A pretty fucking simple one. Yes or no?"

"She doesn't have a discernable one. I mean, she's an Army brat and she spent some time in the South. Every now and then I catch a trace of a twang, but it's nothing to write home about."

"So she's not Australian?"

Mike chuckled. "What the hell are you talking about? Are you drinking already?"

"No. Listen. I gotta go. Talk to you later."

"Are you going to explain—"

Andrew clicked the phone off in the middle of Mike's question.

Who the fuck was upstairs in his bed?

He'd accused her of breaking in, but she'd claimed to have a key. If Mike didn't give it to her, then who did?

Harper. The only other person with a house key was his sister.

Shit.

The Australian teacher.

Harper had mentioned the woman several times in passing over the past year. Something about starting a pen pal program.

He tried to recall if Harper had ever said the woman's

name. He was sure she had, but it simply hadn't stuck. He really needed to work on his paying attention skills.

Great. So now he knew who was in his bed. Problem was he still didn't know why she was there or where Harper was. He reached for his phone once more and dialed his sister's number. It took him straight to voicemail.

"Harper. It's Andrew. Why the fuck is Amy here? And where the fuck are you? Call me back."

He clicked off the phone and cursed his temper. She'd never call him back now.

Andrew retrieved his laptop from the front hall where he'd left it last night and fired it up on the island in the kitchen. Then he pulled over a stool. A quick check of his email confirmed what his producer had said yesterday. Filming would be postponed for not quite a week and if the monsoon did too much damage, they'd have to fall back and punt, find another locale.

Harper had said her so-called conference would last one week. Now he was wondering if that was where she really was. Why would she invite a friend to visit from Australia, then leave town?

She wouldn't.

He racked his brain for an answer, but nothing came. He glanced upward. One person knew what was going on and she was sleeping in the room above his head. Since it didn't appear Harper was going to answer his questions, maybe it was time he and Amy had a little heart-to-heart.

Time for the moment of truth. Climbing the stairs, he headed toward his room.

He was surprised when he spotted Amy, fully dressed and sitting on the edge of his bed, talking on the phone. He paused at the doorway. She hadn't noticed him.

"What the hell am I supposed to tell him?" she asked the other person on the phone.

Him who? Him *him?*

"I understand that, but..." She paused, obviously listening to something the other person was saying. "Okay. I'll try. Yeah. Sure. I promise."

Amy's shoulders sagged as she sighed and he wondered who she was talking to. Was she talking to Harper? About him?

He stepped into the room. Amy's eyes widened when she spotted him.

"Um, listen. I have to go. Give my love to Thomo and Blue. See you later."

She disconnected the phone quickly and turned it off.

"Important phone call?"

She shook her head. "Not really. Just checking in back home." He couldn't help but notice the way her eyes wandered away from his. Amy was a lousy poker player.

"I noticed your suitcase in the guest room."

She nodded, but didn't offer an answer. Her eyes, which had been so warm and friendly last night, seemed leery this morning. He walked across the room, standing in front of her. He casually took her phone from her.

"What are you doing?" she asked, trying to grab it back.

Andrew flicked it on. Fucking security lock. "Who were you talking to?"

"None of your business."

"Sweetheart, you made it my business when you broke into my house and made yourself at home in my bed."

Amy bit her lower lip. He was being an asshole, but he was tired and starting to worry about his sister.

"I told you. I didn't break in. I have a key."

He nodded slowly. "That's right. The key. Who gave it to you?"

"A friend."

Andrew's temper exploded. "Goddamn it, Amy. I'm not playing around. Who gave you the fucking key?"

Apparently he wasn't the only one who'd woken up in a bad mood. Amy rose from the bed, placed her hands on her hips and leaned forward, her gaze narrowed. "Who did you think I was last night?"

Her question caught him unaware. "Someone else."

"Obviously. Do you make it a habit to chain strange women to your bed and fuck them senseless?"

A nasty grin formed. "You weren't exactly fighting me off, angel."

"Funny. Those scratches on your face seem to say differently."

They could spend all day arguing over all the ways last night was wrong…and oh so right. Andrew didn't have time for that.

"You shaved." Her comment took him off guard.

Andrew rubbed his jaw, touching the smooth skin. "So?"

"I recognize you now."

She knew him? "How?"

"I looked you up online. Googled your name and saw a few short clips from your show. I thought your eyes looked familiar last night, but I was jet-lagged and not thinking very clearly. The beard threw me."

"Where's Harper?"

Amy's face lost its color, her flushed cheeks fading to white. "Harper?"

"Don't play stupid. Where's my sister? Is that who you were talking to on the phone?"

Amy released a long sigh and sank on to the mattress. "I don't suppose you'll just take my word when I say she's fine."

He crossed his arms. "You're right. I won't. Tell me where she is."

"She asked me not to. And I promised I wouldn't."

Andrew frowned. "Harper wouldn't do that. We don't keep secrets from each other."

Amy shrugged. "I guess you do now."

He tried to figure out why Harper would skip town without telling him. His mind drifted back to a disagreement they'd had a few weeks earlier. Harper had said something about needing to get away. He'd offered to take her on location with him, but she'd said she was twenty-five and more than capable of taking a vacation on her own. He had tried to convince her it was no fun traveling alone. Eventually she just let the conversation drop and he thought she'd given up on the idea.

Apparently she hadn't.

Andrew sat down on the bed next to Amy. He wasn't making progress with his asshole routine. Time to turn on the charm. He reached out and grasped her hand. Amy accepted it, though suspicion filled her eyes.

"All I'm asking is where she is, Amy. It's not like I'm going to fly off to parts unknown to find her."

"Actually, that's exactly what she said you'll do."

"She's wrong."

Amy gave him a grin he instantly distrusted. "Then why do you need to know where she is?"

His grip tightened. "Is she in the country?"

Amy didn't reply, her gaze holding steady on his, offering him no clue. Why was Amy here when Harper wasn't?

The truth crashed down on him like an avalanche. "Motherfucker. She flew to Australia, didn't she?"

Amy tried to hold steady, but this time, he caught her

slight wince. His sister had taken off halfway across the goddamn planet.

"Where in Australia?"

Amy tried to retrieve her hand, but he refused to let go. "Where?" he repeated. "Is she at your house?"

More silence met his question.

"Fine. I'll find her myself."

"How?" she asked.

He didn't have a clue. He didn't know Amy's last name, didn't have any idea where she lived in Oz, nothing. "You're going to tell me."

She laughed. "I already told you I wouldn't. Australia's a bloody big country, you know? If you're going to go over there to look for her, you better start now. Should only take you a few…dozen years or so."

"Thanks for the geography lesson, but I'm not going off on a wild goose chase. I won't need to. You'll tell me everything I need to know. I can be very persuasive when I need to be."

She didn't bother to respond, her smirk tweaking his nerves. "I'd really love to hang out and chat, but I need to get going. Looks like I need to find a new place to stay since my holiday home is already occupied."

Now it was his turn to grin. "You're not going anywhere. In fact, you're my collateral. Until you tell me where my sister is or until Harper comes home, you're staying right here where I can keep an eye on you. Consider yourself under house arrest."

He expected her to argue, to pitch a fit, to wage a battle similar to the one they'd engaged in the previous evening. His damn cock actually started to thicken at the thought.

He should have known better. Amy hadn't done a

single predictable thing since stripping off her clothes and crawling between his sheets.

Instead, she smiled, looking very pleased by his threat. "Fine. I don't have enough money for a hotel anyway." She stood, though he still kept hold of her hand. "If you'll excuse me, I'll go unpack my things in the guest room."

"Oh. Did I forget to mention? You'll be staying in this room. With me."

Amy feigned a yawn. "Been there, done that."

"And you'll be doing it again."

She started to tug against his grip in earnest, but he held firm. "Not in this lifetime, hotshot. Last night you got lucky because I was tired and not thinking straight. Today's a different game."

"That's right." He twisted her hands behind her back, securing them there in one of his then reaching into the nightstand drawer and pulling out a pair of handcuffs. He snapped then in place easily, despite Amy's struggles. "This game *is* completely new."

AMY'S HEAD SPUN. Andrew was keeping her here? In his room?

And he thought she'd be resistant?

Andrew really didn't understand the difference between punishment and bloody good fun. His high-handed ways were slightly annoying, but they were nothing she couldn't deal with. She'd held her own against Thomo and Blue for years, so this Yank had another thing coming if he thought he was going to run roughshod over her.

Besides, he was playing completely into her hand. She needed a place to stay in Chicago the next two weeks and sharing his king-sized bed would be no hardship. In fact, despite the cuffs at her wrists—how hot were they?—she'd say the morning had turned out much better than she'd expected.

She'd woken up in a full-fledged panic, wondering what the hell she was supposed do. Instinct overpowered intelligence and before she could think through why she shouldn't call Harper, her friend was on the other end of the line.

It had been on the tip of her tongue to confess to the misunderstanding that had led to a night of amazing sex, but Amy wasn't sure how Harper would feel about her friend sleeping with her brother. Besides, Harper sounded so happy and excited, she hated to say anything to ruin her friend's vacation.

Just because she'd epically fucked up everything, there was no reason to take Harper down with her. Instead, she'd simply told her friend that Andrew had returned early. She wasn't sure what she had expected Harper to say, but she was surprised when her friend begged her to continue to hide the fact she was in Australia.

How was Amy supposed to stay in Harper's house without confessing to Andrew who she was? Although she'd suspected—and rightly so—that Andrew would figure it out on his own eventually.

Then Andrew had walked in. One look at his pissed-off face and she'd begun trying to mentally calculate how much money was in her bank account and how high she'd have to charge up her credit cards to foot the bill for a hotel room.

Her conscience nagged, telling her it was wrong to sleep with Harper's brother. Fortunately, she'd always been very good at justifying most of her questionable actions. After all, Harper was forcing her to take this path as Amy was simply trying to protect her friend's secret.

God. She was pathetic.

And still bloody horny.

Andrew had appeared last night with that Zac Efron-looking scruff he'd sported in *The Lucky One* and Amy had been a goner. Even without the short beard, Andrew was entirely too good-looking for her peace of mind.

"Start walking," Andrew said, pushing her toward the doorway. "I'm feeling the need for a hearty breakfast. Gonna have to build up my strength. Then you and I will spend the rest of the day in bed—getting better acquainted in between naps while we recover from our jet lag. By the way, you'll be chained to the headboard. Sound good?"

"Sounds perfect." She struggled not to laugh when Andrew frowned at her response. God, he really was making this all too easy. "And just so you know, you're not going to trick me into telling you anything about where I live."

His grip on her arm tightened. Amy's stomach clenched. She was a sucker for an alpha male.

They walked in silence down the hallway. Amy caught a glimpse of her suitcase in the guest room and felt like dancing. Her trip was saved after all. She wouldn't go broke paying for a hotel room and she would be treated to night after night of nonstop, no-holds-barred sex with Andrew.

Could life get any better?

As they approached the kitchen, the sweet smell of coffee drew her straight to the counter. "If I promise to behave, will you take the handcuffs off and let me have a cup of coffee? Even hardcore prisoners get bread and water, you know."

Andrew studied her face as she tried to hide her absolute glee. "Fuck. You're going to be a pain in my ass, aren't you?"

She winked at him.

Andrew chuckled as he released the cuffs. "Coffee cups are in the cabinet above the dishwasher. Help yourself. Gotta warn you. It's strong."

She was surprised—and disappointed—by his easy capitulation. She was hoping for more of a fight.

Andrew grabbed a skillet and placed it on the stove. Then he rummaged around in the refrigerator, bending over in search of something. She enjoyed the view of his arse as the material of his pants stretched and outlined it. She was almost sorry when he found the bacon and eggs. He turned around too quickly and caught her staring.

He lifted an eyebrow. "Enjoying the show?"

She ignored his arrogant comment, turning back toward the cabinet to find a mug. "Strong coffee sounds perfect. My head's still fuzzy from so much travel. And sex."

He chuckled. "Then we're in the same boat."

"Harper expected you to be away for a few weeks. What happened?"

He didn't look happy at her mention of his sister. For a second she thought he might start questioning her again, hit her with a more intense third degree. Fortunately, he let it go. Though she had no doubt he'd badger her relentlessly later.

Harper was perfectly safe and having a great time. There was no harm in keeping her friend's secret and having a bit of fun with her sexy brother along the way.

Andrew reached for a bowl, then cracked several eggs before stirring them with a whisk. Amy tried to decide if there was anything hotter than a shirtless man making her breakfast. "I spent two days traveling toward a monsoon before my producers realized that was a stupid thing to do."

"Clever producers." Amy took a sip of the coffee and

winced. She wasn't much of a coffee drinker and he wasn't kidding about it being strong. He must've noticed her reaction.

"There's creamer in the fridge and sugar on the counter if you want to cut that some."

"What the hell is creamer?"

He lifted one shoulder. "It's like milk."

"So why don't you just say milk?"

He shook his head, his expression the perfect mix of exasperation and humor. "I have no idea."

She grinned, then accepted his offer. "Your job must be incredible. Traveling all over the world, seeing so many amazing places. I'm so bloody jealous, I can hardly see straight."

Andrew's face brightened as he threw some bacon in the pan to fry. His carefree expression reminded her of the man she'd slept with last night. He and Harper shared a striking family resemblance, with their dark complexions and crystal-blue eyes. "I'm not going to lie. It's the greatest way to make a living. You travel much?"

She shook her head. "Actually, this is my first time out of Australia."

"No way. I've been to Australia a few times with the show. I'll admit there are some definite differences as far as the landscape goes. The red of the Outback, the lush green of the Tasmanian rainforests, the sapphire of the Blue Mountains, the fluorescent cityscape of the Gold Coast. Depending on where you're from, of course. Do you find that to be true of your hometown? Does it have a color?"

He paused, clearly expecting her to answer.

"Really, Andrew? So obvious. So lame. I'm not telling you where Harper is."

He shrugged good-naturedly. "Can't blame a guy for

trying. So what do you think of our country?" Andrew put down the whisk and leaned against the counter.

She licked her lips and tilted her head in what she hoped was a seductive pose. "I've enjoyed the Chicago hospitality so far."

Mercifully, the sexy man took her hint. Reaching over, he pulled the pan from the heat and turned the stove off. "How hungry are you?"

She unbuttoned her blouse, loving the way Andrew's gaze devoured her as she pulled the soft material over her shoulders. She hadn't bothered putting her bra back on in her haste to cover up earlier. "I'm starving."

A quick glance at Andrew's track pants confirmed he was ready to roll. His thick cock was hard and leaving an impressive tent in the cotton. "Amy—"

"Gettin' cold feet? And here I was thinking you were this big tough guy," she taunted when she sensed his hesitation.

"Take off those pants and bend over the table."

His commanding tone pushed every bloody hot button she had. She quickly complied, positioning herself so that he had a bird's-eye view of her arse, the one he'd called gorgeous last night.

Andrew started to pull his pants down, then cursed. "Fuck. Condoms are upstairs."

Amy began to rise but he pressed her back against the smooth wood. "No. Don't move. Not an inch. I want you to stay exactly like this, waiting for me."

"Don't take too long."

He placed a light slap on her arse for her cheekiness, though there was no pain associated with the action. It was meant to serve as a reminder, nothing more.

She pressed her legs together, feeling the wetness coating the insides of her thighs.

"Actually," Andrew said, "I want you to wait for me with your legs open." He tapped his toes against her ankles until they were spread apart enough to suit him.

"You realize you could have already gotten the bloody condom and been back by now." His stalling was making her cranky.

"Maybe so, but eventually you need to learn that anticipation makes the reward a lot sweeter."

She groaned when he moved away from the table, but didn't bother to leave the room.

Here we go again.

He was going to play with her body until it felt like it would explode with unrequited lust.

"Please, Andrew. Let's just have a quickie. To take the edge off. Then you can tease me all you want."

Andrew didn't reply. He reached toward a basket on the counter, grabbing a wooden spoon. That wasn't on the list of limits.

Not that it mattered. She wasn't about to turn down anything. She still regretted saying Oz and missing her opportunity to explore anal sex.

"You don't mind pain."

She remained quiet. His comment had been rhetorical. She wasn't going to waste the breath denying something that was obvious to both of them.

"In fact, it makes you hot."

He returned to the table, standing directly behind her arse. She couldn't see him without lifting her head and twisting. She didn't bother. Listening to his deep voice, while not being able to see him or what he planned to do, added to the excitement. She'd told him she wouldn't call him master, but she had to admit, he was bloody good at mastering her.

"How hot can I make you, Amy?"

She bit her lip to keep from telling him she was already in danger of spontaneous combustion and he hadn't laid a finger on her. Before she could offer any answer, the wooden spoon landed squarely on her arse.

She yelped with surprise and pain. "Bloody hell."

He repeated the action. Once, twice, three times more. She squeezed her eyes shut, her fingers white-knuckling the edge of the table. The spoon disappeared, the pain of it being washed away by the sheer bliss of his fingers as he pressed them inside her pussy. She lifted up on her toes, struggling for more of his deep, powerful thrusts. Sweat gathered at her brow as the heat from her arse and her pussy mingled, driving her arousal closer to the flames she hoped would consume her.

His fingers disappeared before she could leap onto the pyre. Bloody bastard was up to his same tricks. "You fucking arsehole."

He chuckled, swatting her with the spoon several more times. Each blow landed somewhere different and with a varying amount of power. She never knew what to expect as some were gentle taps, others painful slaps.

When his fingers returned to her weeping pussy, she pressed her forehead against the table, seeking some coolness from the wood. Andrew leaned over her as he continued to fuck her, his fingers driving inside her relentlessly. Mercifully, he didn't stop and Amy stiffened as an orgasm rumbled through her body.

"Mother. Fuck. Shit. Bloody hell." Every curse she'd ever heard flew from her lips in a long stream as tremors shook her.

Andrew's fingers stilled, though he kept them buried deep. "Where's my sister?" he whispered.

"Oz."

She let the word hover in the air between them. It

would be up to him to decide if that was her answer or her retreat. He lay on top of her for several long moments as she tried to catch her breath.

When Andrew rose, he placed a kiss in the middle of her back. "Stay put."

She wanted to laugh, but she didn't have the energy. She wasn't going anywhere and he knew it. He'd fucked her boneless. Again.

She closed her eyes, listening to the pounding of her heart. She was so replete and exhausted, she failed to hear Andrew when he returned to the kitchen.

The sound of the condom package tearing caught her attention. Her eyelids drifted open just as the head of his cock nudged against her pussy, seeking entrance. She thought she was too done in to do much more than simply go along for the ride. But she was mistaken. Andrew wasn't content to let her be the passive observer as he found his pleasure in her body. He'd yet to allow her to be a wall-flower at *his* party.

His fingers found her clit, rubbing with enough pres-sure to rouse a flame from what she thought were dying embers. She groaned, fresh moisture easing his path as he pushed deep.

"Jesus, Amy."

She loved the way her name sounded in his American accent. *A-mee.* Andrew's thrusts were slow at first, but soon his pace increased, dragging her arousal along with it. She pressed the palms of her hands against the tabletop, trying to find purchase as she countered with an assault of her own. He was taking her with a might that spoke of his own overwhelming need. Desire gave way to greediness.

"God. Fuck me harder, Andrew. Deeper."

His hands gripped her hips tightly, pulling her into his plunges. Stars formed behind her eyes.

"Yes," she hissed.

Andrew grasped a handful of her hair, using his hold to pull her upright. He continued to pummel her with hard shoves while he gripped her breast with his free hand, squeezing the sensitive flesh until she cried out.

Her second orgasm took her by surprise, flashing hard and fast. Andrew joined her, yelling out with his own release. Both of them froze, their joined bodies creating an erotic statue as they struggled to return to normal.

What was normal anymore? A week ago, she was a lonely schoolteacher in Australia who spent most nights masturbating to fantasies she thought were scandalous and wicked, but that now seemed lukewarm and unimaginative compared to Andrew's lessons.

If *that* was normal, she'd sell her soul to the devil to avoid returning to her old life, to being that woman.

Andrew slowly pulled out, taking a step away when he was certain she'd found her footing. He placed a gentle hand on her back, the gesture one of protection and care.

"Okay?"

She turned to face him, nodding. "Sort of nice to confirm last night wasn't a fluke or a lucky first attempt."

Andrew laughed, the happy sound filling the quiet room. "Yeah. That's good to know. Even so, I don't think we should rest on our laurels. Might need to try that another dozen or so times just to be sure."

Now it was her turn to laugh. "Cocky bastard."

"Let's eat and take that nap. Then we'll see just how cocky I am." As he spoke, he wrapped her hand around his dick. She was surprised to realize it was already starting to stiffen again.

Captivity certainly had its advantages.

Chapter Four

Andrew followed Amy into the house, watching as she dropped her souvenir bags on a chair in the foyer. He was probably the worst kidnapper in history. His far too willing captive still wouldn't tell him where his sister was, and after spending most of yesterday in bed, alternating between sleep and sex, Amy had roused him early this morning, insisting that he take her sightseeing.

He'd grumbled about playing tourist in his hometown, but he'd eventually given in, gotten dressed and taken her around the city. His little Australian handful was slowly wrapping him around her little finger, something no woman—with the exception of Harper—had ever been able to do.

He'd anticipated being bored all day, but seeing Chicago through Amy's awestruck eyes had rejuvenated his love for the place. Her interest in the history of the city was genuine and he'd actually learned a few things he didn't know. She hadn't lied about doing her homework prior to traveling. Several times during the day, she'd consulted her list, checking off different sights after their visit. Her efficiency was mind-boggling.

Her enthusiasm as she explored Chicago made him realize he'd become jaded lately. He used to feel the same rush Amy had every time he stepped off the plane in a new country, but that passion had been absent on the past few trips. He was currently in contract negotiations with the cable company that produced his show and he'd spent several sleepless nights in the last month trying to decide if he wanted to continue.

One day exploring a city he knew better than the back of his hand with Amy had given him the kick in the pants he'd needed, proven to him he still possessed that same sense of wonder. He wasn't ready to retire yet.

Andrew glanced at the grandfather clock. It was nearly nine. Damn. Talk about making a day of it. They'd boarded the train, heading into the city at eight this morning. Amy had been tireless, practically bouncing from one landmark to the next. He couldn't understand it. She had to be suffering from serious jet lag like him.

"How old are you?" he asked.

She gave him a funny look. "Where did that question come from?"

He shrugged. "No idea. Just dawned on me that I don't know."

"I'm twenty-five, same as Harper. And you're thirty-five, ten years older."

He grimaced. "You seem to know more about me than I do about you."

Amy slipped off her shoes. She'd only been in his childhood home two days, but it already felt like she belonged here. He suspected she was one of those people who were at ease anywhere. "Harper talks about you all the time. Didn't she ever mention me?"

Andrew gave her a guilty look. "She talked about you quite a bit. I just wasn't as good at paying attention as you were. Truth be told, I never anticipated meeting you."

Amy laughed. "Typical male. Only listen if it directly pertains to you. Keith and Marc are exactly the same. I swear I have to repeat myself three or four times before anything sinks into their thick skulls."

"Keith and Marc?" He'd heard her mention the same men earlier in the day as she'd searched for souvenirs.

"My mates back home. They're the ones looking after Harper right now."

He scowled.

"Don't worry, Shaw. They'll take *really* good care of her." She threw a little too much emphasis into her reassurance. Damn Aussie enjoyed trying to get a rise out of him.

"Yeah, well, you'd better hope for their sake they take care of her just enough, but not too much."

"Actually, I have a little bit of a confession to make."

He narrowed his gaze. "About your friends?"

"No," she said, giggling. "About you. I used to pump Harper for information about you all the time."

"Why?"

She lifted one shoulder. "At first I wanted to hear about your adventures at work, the places you were going, stuff like that. But she always added in extra details without realizing it, personality things."

"What sort of things?"

"Like how you're overprotective of her. How you call her almost every single day to check up on her."

He sighed. "I haven't spoken to my sister in three days."

"I know, but I truly believe you need to give Harper this time, this space."

"Why?"

She bit her lower lip. "I don't know why exactly. I just know that Harper was looking forward to escaping her real life for a little while. It's not that she doesn't love you. Honest. She adores you. I don't have a brother, but I always used to think that if I did, I'd want him to be just like you."

"Great." Andrew winced. "So you see me as a brother figure?"

Amy laughed. "Bloody hell, no. I may be a country hick from out Whoop Whoop, but we're not into incest."

"Aha. So my sister isn't in Sydney."

Amy didn't look concerned. "Oh yeah. That really narrows it down for you. All I'm saying is I used to wish I had a brother like you. Then Harper told me some more, um, personal stuff and my brother fantasy morphed into one that was a lot dirtier."

"Dirtier than what we've been indulging in the past two nights? Details."

Her smile remained. Amy was far more forthright than most women he'd been with in the past. She didn't possess a single ounce of modesty.

"Harper sort of let it slip that you belong to a sex club."

Andrew closed his eyes. "How in the hell did that come up in conversation?"

"I told her I wanted to visit one when I came to America."

He thought he was beyond the point where anything Amy said surprised him. He was wrong. "Why?"

Her eyes widened with excitement. "Why not?"

He sighed. Why not indeed?

Her face was still flushed from the chilly evening air. She looked vibrant, healthy, beautiful. Despite his bone-deep weariness, nothing was going to stop him from taking Amy to bed, stripping off her clothing and losing himself in her body. He'd spent most of the day flying at half-mast thanks to her skin-tight jeans and the game of cleavage peekaboo her blouse had played with him. Hell, she even smelled good. Every time he caught a whiff of her citrus-y perfume, he'd been forced to readjust his pants.

Amy, the little minx, had known all about his pained condition and went out of her way to make it worse by *accidentally* brushing against his dick with her ass or her hand no less than a dozen times. She'd treated him to a healthy dose of his own medicine after lunch when he'd suggested they cut the sightseeing short and catch the next train home. She'd given him a wicked grin, pointing out that "anticipation makes the reward sweeter".

Even now, she appeared to be in no hurry to move their party to the bedroom. Instead, she walked straight toward the kitchen. He followed, watching as she pulled a couple beers from the fridge.

"Want one?" she asked, holding them up.

He nodded. "Sure."

Uncapping the Bud Lights, she tapped her bottle against his before taking a sip. She winced. "What the hell is this? Tastes like piss."

"Harper likes it. I prefer Blue Moon myself. Let's see. You're an Aussie girl, so I'm guessing you'd prefer—"

She held up her hand. "If you say Foster's, I will grab my suitcase and walk out of this house right now."

He rolled his eyes. "I was actually going to guess Carlton Draught or maybe VB."

"Wow. Very good, Mr. Shaw. I'm a Toohey's fan, but I'm impressed with your knowledge of Australian beer."

He shrugged. "Like I said yesterday, I've been to your continent three times thanks to work. I hope you won't take this the wrong way. It's a great place to visit, but I wouldn't want to live there."

Her hands flew to her hips, defensively, angrily. There was no doubt Amy was proud of her country. Last night he'd been treated to a glimpse of her pajamas, a tank and panty set that sported the Australian flag.

"What's wrong with Australia?"

He raised his hand, counting off on his fingers as he made his list. "It was ungodly hot. Something tells me it would be cooler living on the sun."

"It's not always hot. The winters can get downright cold. Not Australia's fault you were a bloody dickhead who traveled there in the summer. I think we already determined that your producers are a bunch of tools."

"Fine." He lifted a second finger. "The spiders there are bigger than our goddamn cats."

She laughed. "Not a fan of spiders?"

He faked a shudder. "Not at all."

"Good to know my American Superman has a Kryptonite. I'll have to remember that." Amy claimed a seat at the kitchen table, so he joined her.

He took another sip of beer before continuing his list. "The air is filled with the scent of eucalyptus. Reminded me of the nasty stuff my mother used to rub on my chest when I had a head cold."

"Are you kidding? If I had to name the number one thing I'm missing about home right now, it's that smell."

"Guess you never have to worry about stuffy noses."

"I prefer the fresh, cool honey scent of eucalyptus to your smoggy, sewage-y city smell."

"Hey now. Chicago doesn't stink."

She crinkled her nose. "Maybe not to you."

"Fair enough," he conceded. "It sounds like you and I

are just going to have to agree to disagree about whose country smells the best."

She picked at the label on her beer bottle. He noticed she hadn't taken another sip. He'd probably end up finishing his beer and hers. "You know," she said at last, "Oz is my home and I love it more than vegemite, but I'd leave it in an instant to do a job like yours."

"You'd want to travel for a living?"

She nodded. "There are so many places I'm dying to see. This will probably sound weird, but when I was eleven, the number one thing on my Christmas list was a subscription to a travel magazine. I started to catalog all the cities and countries I wanted to travel to in year eight of school."

"I don't think there's anything strange about that. I have a travel list of my own."

"At least you're making progress on yours. This trip is my first and, given my rather limited income, I think it will probably be my last for years."

Her comment made him realize how little he actually knew about Amy. "That's right. You're a teacher. Like Harper. Guess they're underpaid all over the world."

She hesitated for a moment, then replied with more detail than he'd expected. "I'm a teacher on a cattle station."

"That's like a ranch, right?"

"Except it's a station," she teased. "Full of jackaroos and stockmen. Not a cowboy in sight."

"Gotcha." He took another swig of beer. "Sounds like an interesting place to live. I haven't seen an Aussie cattle station on my travels. Maybe I need to add that to my list."

"If you ever want a tour, just ring me up. I think my bosses would get a kick out of being on American TV." Amy looked around the kitchen. "Although my little cottage is nowhere near as nice as your house."

"It's more accurate to say this is Harper's house. I'm not here more than a dozen weeks or so each year. The rest of the time, I'm either on the road or at my own apartment in L.A. Feels sort of odd to be here this week without her. Unlike you, my sister has an aversion to traveling."

"I know she hasn't done a lot of it, but she was super excited about traveling to Oz."

"Really?" Andrew frowned, wondering when Harper had started changing. The sister he knew would never drop everything for two weeks to head off for parts unknown alone. He could only assume Amy had been a big influence on her. That wasn't necessarily a bad thing. He worried about Harper's introverted ways.

He and his sister were long overdue for a chat. "Usually she's a homebody. While she's done some traveling in the States, she's never ventured into another country, with the exception of the time our family went to Niagara Falls in Canada. Even then, she was only little. I doubt she even remembers it."

Amy noticed his empty beer bottle and handed hers to him with a grin. "Harper loves you, Andrew, but that doesn't mean she has to tell you everything."

Damn. So much for his poker face. Amy must've recognized his concern. "I used to think we were really close. This secret trip of hers is throwing me for a loop."

"She's a big girl. Heading out on her own is probably a good thing for both of you."

He knew his sister was an adult, but that didn't make it any easier for him to let go. There was too much history between them, too many painful memories. "Harper's the most important person in my life. We tend to cling to each other, considering our family fell firmly within the dysfunctional category. Did she tell you she's actually my half-sister?"

"No. She didn't. What do you mean by dysfunctional?"

He stretched out in the chair, leaning back, grateful for the downtime. He felt like he'd run a marathon today rather than merely going sightseeing with Amy. "My parents were married for several years before they had me, then my mom died when I was eight."

"Oh Andrew. I'm sorry."

"Cancer."

Amy reached over and grasped his hand, squeezing it. "That's what got my dad too. Just a couple years ago."

Her kindness touched him, made him want to open up to her. Typically his past was one of those books that remained firmly closed. He hadn't spoken about his parents in years. "My dad waited all of four months after burying my mother before he married his secretary. Dad and the secretary had Harper, which is why I'm ten years older than her. She's the product of a second marriage."

"The secretary? She doesn't have a name?"

Andrew hadn't called the woman by her given name in years, and he was using the term secretary to keep things clean for Amy. Truth was nowadays he usually thought of his stepmother as *that whore* or *the bitch*. It was one of the reasons he never talked about family matters, especially with Harper. He never wanted his sister to know how much he despised her mother, even though he suspected the feeling was somewhat mutual.

"Her name's Sarah." He swallowed heavily, the word leaving a dirty taste in his mouth.

"You hate her."

He didn't bother to deny it. "Yeah. I do."

"Why?"

He wasn't going down that road. Ever again, if he could help it. "She wasn't a very nice person. She cheated on my dad, then left him and married an asshole."

"Harper stayed with you and your dad?"

He shook his head. She should have. His father should have moved heaven and earth to get custody of Harper. If he *had*…

Andrew shut the thought down before it could form.

"She lived with her mom for almost a year, but it didn't work out." *That's the understatement of the century.* "That's when she came to stay with me and our dad. Then Dad had a heart attack when Harper was fourteen. I was in my early twenties, out of school and working, so she just stayed with me."

"Wow. Sounds like you were her brother, mother and father rolled into one."

Andrew picked up Amy's beer and drained it in one long swig. Her concerned gaze made him uncomfortable and he was worried she'd keep asking questions, continue picking at things better left alone.

Thankfully, she let it go. "I'm afraid my family story will seem boring in comparison. My parents were married until my dad passed away, at which point, my mum moved to Sydney to be closer to my older sisters and their families. I was the baby, which means at heart, I'm terribly spoiled and used to getting my own way."

Andrew pretended to be shocked. "You? Spoiled?"

She lightly punched his arm and they fell into a companionable silence. Andrew relaxed, content to merely sit and talk to her. He couldn't remember the last time he'd had a conversation with a woman other than his sister. Mike was right. He'd been stuck in a rut of work and sex club affairs. He hadn't realized what he was missing until Amy climbed into his bed.

"So where's that sightseeing list of yours? I want to know how much other shit I'm going to have to endure this week." While Amy had consulted it regularly, he hadn't seen it himself.

She reached into the back pocket of her jeans and pulled it out. "You loved every minute and you know it. But don't worry. We made progress today."

He took it from her and unfolded the sheet of paper. She'd drawn lines through Skydeck and the aquarium, as well as the Museum of Contemporary Art. He couldn't believe how much they'd managed to squeeze into one day. She still wanted to go to the Navy Pier. The other places on her list were typical tourist attractions. There were a couple he'd try to talk her out of because they just weren't worth the time. Finally his gaze landed on the last item on the list.

She wanted to go to Velvet Chains.

"No," he muttered. He should have known he'd find it on the list. After all, she'd already confessed her interest in going to a sex club and that Harper had told her about his membership.

"What?" she asked.

"I'll take you to every single one of these places if you'll mark Velvet Chains off your list."

"Why?"

He knew why, but he wasn't willing to tell her. "I'm sure Harper's built it up as this really cool place, but I don't think you'd like it there."

"Why not?"

"Just mark it off your list."

She shook her head. "No. I want to go there."

Shit. This was going to turn into an argument if he didn't take a giant step back. He'd simply have to keep her so busy doing other things that she wouldn't have time for Velvet Chains.

Of course, that solution would only work until he left town and she was on her own next week.

"You don't have to take me there if you don't want to. I never intended to have a tour guide for any of this stuff. I'm fine going on my own."

Did she really think that would make him feel better? "We'll talk about it later."

Amy looked determined to finish the conversation now. "Andrew—"

"Stand up." He'd waited all day to take her. His patience had officially run out.

Amy glanced around the room and graced him with a mischievous grin. "Kitchen again?"

The idea of stretching her out over the table once more had its merits.

"No." He preferred taking her in the comfort of his own bed, seeing her displayed, naked on his silk sheets. The sheets were an indulgence, one that Harper gave him shit for. She'd called him a player when he'd first brought them home, despite the fact he hadn't invited a woman back to their house in years. Amy was the first to sleep between those sheets with him.

Together they stood and Andrew grasped her hand. As they walked through the foyer, he picked up his single bag of purchases. He'd insisted on only one stop as they'd toured the city. A sex shop. They'd spent nearly an hour picking out the bagful of toys.

She laughed when he grabbed the bag and started up the stairs. "I think it's going to be a very good night."

"Strip," he commanded when they entered his room.

Amy unfastened her jeans, shimmying them off. "What about you?" she asked, as he watched her without removing any clothing.

"I'll get there. Eventually. Continue."

Amy wasted no time removing the rest of her clothes. He loved her lack of reserve, her seductive poise. Confidence radiated from her. Andrew had never realized how sexy that trait was.

"Why do you belong to a sex club?"

He sighed. She wasn't going to let the argument go. "When I was younger, I discovered I had a taste for BDSM."

"Let me guess. You're the Dom."

Andrew laughed. "Usually. I'll admit you've been giving me a run for my money."

"Is that why you won't take me to Velvet Chains? Because you're worried I'll give away the fact that you're really a giant teddy bear."

"Jesus. Is that what you think of me? Looks like I need to step up my game."

She ran her hand along the bedspread. "Actually, I like it when you take control. Doesn't that make me a submissive?"

He shook his head. "You have submissive qualities, but no, I don't think you'll ever truly be someone's sub."

She frowned. "I disagree."

Whether Amy knew it or not, she was presenting a challenge he found impossible to resist. "When I ask for something, I expect it to be done without question or hesitation."

"Oooh. Yes Sir." She struck a pose he was sure she meant to be silly, but it looked far too sexy for his aching libido. No one tested his ability to go slowly like Amy.

"Amy—"

"I took off my clothes when you asked."

"Fine. You want a demonstration? Go sit in the middle of the bed. Place your back against the headboard."

Her face brightened as she climbed on the bed. He

almost hated to prove she was wrong. She definitely liked the idea of pleasing him. So long as it pleased her too. She was too headstrong to ever truly submit. In the past that information would have been a red flag for him. A sign for him to move on.

Right now, it was more temptation than he could resist.

He walked to the foot of the bed as Amy took the position he requested. "Open your legs."

Again, she obeyed.

"Are you wet?"

She nodded. "Bloody oath."

He narrowed his gaze. "You had it right before. The correct answer is 'Yes Sir'."

Amy hesitated, her face showing how much that little response bothered her when it wasn't being spoken in jest. Then she licked her lips and said, "Yes Sir."

He fought to restrain his grin. That had rubbed against the grain.

He forged on, wanting to see how far he could push her. "Lift your breasts up."

This time she reacted without a thought. His Aussie wildcat had no inhibitions about displaying herself to him. Her breasts were firm and full, the perfect complement to her narrow waist and round hips. The term "hourglass figure" could have been coined for her.

"Pinch your nipples."

She complied.

"Harder."

Her fingers tightened on her own flesh. He crawled along the middle of the mattress toward her.

Amy's gaze captured his, never wavering as he hovered over her on his hands and knees.

"Feed that pretty tit to me."

She lifted her breast toward his mouth. Andrew sucked

it in, enjoying Amy's soft sigh. She reached up to touch him, her fingers running through his hair as she pressed him tighter to her chest.

He released her nipple with a pop. "Leave your hands on your breasts."

Her hands lingered. She wanted to be an active participant, so it was hard for her to let got of the steering wheel. She'd never relinquish control to him. His gaze held hers, letting her know he wouldn't touch her until she obeyed.

She dropped her hands back to her breasts slowly, lifting them up. He rewarded her with a quick kiss on the cheek. Then he resumed his place at her nipple, sucking on the tight nub until she groaned.

"God, Andrew. That feels so bloody good."

He turned his head and administered the same treatment to the other breast as Amy held it for him. When he was able to force himself away, he leaned back on his haunches. He reached for the bag of toys he'd dropped on the edge of the bed, pulling out the nipple clamps he'd bought for her.

She sucked in a deep breath when he turned back to her, bending his head and taking her nipple into his mouth. This time he teased the nub with his teeth as well as his tongue until it was taut. She gasped when he put the first clamp on, but she didn't complain and—thank God—didn't use her safe word.

He repeated the motions on her other breast, then sat back to study his work.

Amy's face was flushed. Her eyes fluttered open, her forehead crinkling at his departure. "Don't stop. It feels good."

He didn't move. Instead, he let his gaze drift lower. "Open yourself up. Let me see that sweet pussy."

She blinked rapidly. He thought for a moment she

would protest his retreat. He raised his eyebrow and, once again, waited her out.

She mumbled something incoherent under her breath and he tried not to laugh. If he were at the club with one of his subs, the woman would have been turned over his knee after the first hesitation, but he was trying to prove a point to Amy about her lack of submissive tendencies. He wondered which was stronger. Her determination to win their argument or the part of her that didn't bend its will to anyone.

"Fine," she muttered. Her fingers drifted to her pussy. He watched as she slowly rubbed her clit, obviously intent on taking matters into her own hands…literally.

"I didn't tell you to touch your clit. Just to hold yourself open." He purposely made his tone deep, demanding.

She bit her lip, no doubt to keep from reading him the riot act. Then she slowly opened herself to his gaze. She wasn't offended by his commands. Her cunt was shiny with juice from her aroused body.

"Now, I need to do a couple things. While you're waiting for me to return, I want you to stick two fingers inside all that wet heat and stroke yourself. Slowly. Don't touch your clit and don't come."

She frowned. "Where are you going?"

"Did I give you permission to speak?"

His question had the desired effect. "Listen, you bloody arsehole, I'm sitting here in agony because you won't pull your thumb out and fuck me. If I want to bitch about that—"

He cut her tirade off with a quick, hard kiss. Then he grasped her wrist, opened the hand she'd clenched into a fist and pushed two of her fingers inside her pussy. "That wasn't so hard, was it?"

She would have killed him—he saw murder flash in her

eyes—if he hadn't distracted her by stroking her clit.

He continued to play with her until her hips began gyrating, seeking more friction. Then he moved away, climbing off the bed.

Amy released a loud groan. "God, I hate you."

He chuckled. "No, you don't. Be a good girl, Amy, and I'll give you everything you want."

"Fine. Hurry up."

It was his turn to take a steadying breath. Sex with her was a challenge to his control. He admired her spirit, yet he still felt the need to hold the reins. It was tough to find the middle ground where they'd both be satisfied.

He reached out and touched the tiny weight attached to one of the nipple clamps, tugging on it with just enough pressure to produce a bit of pain. She gasped.

"Behave," he repeated.

Amy's pupils dilated, her nostrils flared, and then, mercifully, she nodded.

Progress.

He carried the rest of his purchases to the bathroom, removing the wrappings and washing them all. He'd spared no expense because he knew his time with Amy was limited. They only had a few more nights together and there was too damn much he wanted to do with her. *To* her.

When he returned to the room, he was relieved to see she hadn't moved, hadn't disobeyed him. Her hand moved slowly inside her pussy. While her fingers kept the fire stoked, it wasn't enough to push her over.

He dropped the cleaned toys as well as a new tube of lubrication on the mattress, then started to disrobe. Amy's gaze never left his body as he calmly removed his shirt, his shoes and socks, his pants.

She licked her lips, devouring him with her hungry

eyes. Her passion was contagious. His cock had been rock hard and aching since they'd returned from the train station. He wasn't sure how much longer he could hold off. All he knew was he needed to take this slow. He'd mentally charted tonight's activities after leaving the sex shop. He was determined to see it through.

Once he was naked, he returned to the bed. Gripping her by her knees, he pulled until she lay flat on her back.

The sudden movement took her by surprise and her hands flew up to grip him by his shoulders.

"Ready for more?"

She grinned at his question. "That's rhetorical, right?"

He lifted her legs until her knees were pressed high, near her shoulders. "Hold your legs there. Just like that."

She grabbed her knees as he enjoyed the view she provided.

Picking up the lube, he uncapped it and smeared some on his finger. Then he pressed it against her anus. He froze for a moment and waited. "You remember your safe word?"

She nodded.

"You want to say it?"

She shook it. "No. I don't."

"You've never been fucked here, right?"

Again, she shook her head.

"I'm going to."

She swallowed visibly. "I want you to."

He pushed his finger in, letting the lube ease his way. Once she'd adjusted to one finger, he added more lube and another. Her breathing accelerated. He kept a close eye on her face, waiting for some sign that she was in pain, unhappy. The emotions never came. Instead she urged him on, asking him to move faster, to go deeper.

Jesus. It took all the strength in his body not to pull his

fingers out and slam inside her. To set himself free, to release the bonds on his hard-earned control. What would it feel like? To give himself over to her completely without holding anything back?

He dismissed the thought. This wasn't the time. She wasn't the woman. She couldn't be. They had one week. Seven days in paradise before the real world would return, intrude, drive them apart. He couldn't let this go any further than the here and now. Sex without emotion. Passion tempered by restraint. He was a master of that. It was all he'd ever known.

So why did this feel like more?

"Andrew. Please." Her fingers were digging into the backs of her legs as she continued to hold herself open to his exploration.

He removed his fingers, not giving her a chance to complain before he grabbed the butt plug from the mattress. He slathered it in lube, then pushed it inside her ass slowly.

"Fuck," she cried out. "Yes."

The sight of her, flushed with arousal, wearing his clamps, her ass full, was more than he could stand. The leash he held on his control slipped, fell away.

"Hold your breath." He only gave her a split second to do so as he released one nipple clamp and then the other.

Amy yelled out, and he recognized the second the pain gave way to pleasure. Her hips lifted from the bed as she sought satisfaction. "God, Andrew. Need you. Now."

He wrapped his lips around one nipple, sucking it deeply as he massaged the other with his hand. Her hands tangled in his hair, pulling it so hard his scalp burned. He'd never been the recipient of discomfort, always keeping his lovers tied up so they couldn't touch him.

Is that what was so different about her? She touched

him. And not just physically. He tightened the suction, determined to drive the wayward thought from his mind. This was just sex.

He pushed himself away, caging her beneath him on the mattress.

Her gaze captured his and he saw it—Amy felt the same things. His spunky Aussie was waging the same internal battle.

"We only have a week." Her voice was so quiet that, despite their closeness, he could almost pretend she hadn't spoken at all.

"It will have to be enough." He didn't know what else to say. He had nothing to offer her. He didn't do relationships. His job didn't afford him that luxury.

She gave him a small smile. "We'll make it enough." With her words, she wrapped her legs around his waist, pulling him down until his cock touched her opening. The plug still filled her ass, making his entrance harder, tighter.

"Condom." He'd almost forgotten. He'd never forgotten.

"Birth control. Please don't stop."

"Amy." It was too much.

It wasn't enough.

He pushed inside, trying to block out the exquisite agony. She was tight. He was bare. Had he ever felt anything more incredible? Fuck. One shove and he was going to blow like Old Faithful.

"I'm afraid this won't take long."

She laughed. "Good. I hate to come alone."

It was all he needed to hear. He stroked her clit as he thrust inside her. Amy gripped his shoulders, urging him on with her cries.

He hadn't exaggerated. His balls began to tighten after only a minute or so. He was a goner. Luckily Amy was true to her word as well. Her inner muscles clenched, squeezing his dick tightly. He suddenly understood the meaning of *hurt so good*.

He came with a loud groan, his come filling her tight passage.

"So. Bloody. Good," she said as he lifted himself away and fell to her side.

He grinned at her accent, her labored breathing. He was struggling to push air into his own lungs. His skin was slick with sweat and his heart was racing so hard he thought it might burst. He couldn't deny the truth of her words, so he gave it back to her. In her own language. "That was bloody awesome."

She laughed at his exaggerated attempt at sounding Australian. "Submissive enough?"

He rolled his eyes. "You're kidding, right?"

She shrugged, her face betraying she knew just how bad a submissive she was. "You know, I suck at Algebra too, but I had a great teacher who didn't give up on me. She gave me extra problems to do and we drilled and drilled until it became easier."

"You seriously want to learn to be a submissive?" For some reason the idea didn't rest well with him.

"I don't know. Maybe you're right. Maybe I don't have what it takes. I just like the idea of you and me practicing some more. You know, drilling."

Andrew laughed. God. She was a piece of work. "I could be on board for a few more lessons, misplaced though they may be. After all, drilling is one of my strong suits."

He pulled her close and kissed her. He'd never cuddled with a woman after sex, but holding Amy felt natural. Right.

Shit.

Chapter Five

Amy lay on the couch and stretched lazily. She was fairly certain she'd never had a better day than today. Hell, she'd never had a bloody *week* as phenomenal as this one. Andrew had been the ultimate tour guide, enduring not just one, but two days of nonstop sightseeing with her. After their first marathon day, she'd expected him to beg off on going back into the city again.

Then he'd surprised her by waking her up early yesterday morning for round two of the tours. They'd spent a wonderful morning at Navy Pier, then devoted the afternoon to marking three more things off her to-do list.

Only one thing remained—Velvet Chains.

Andrew seemed determined to keep their sexual explorations private, refusing to take her to the sex club, though he wouldn't tell her why.

Today, she'd granted him a reprieve. They'd opted for a long sleep-in—intermingled with sex, sex and more sex. Then they had a late breakfast and spent the morning hanging out around the house.

She glanced at the TV and grinned as Andrew's image

stood with Hurricane Ridge in the background, talking about the area, the mountain ranges in the distance and why it was on his list of best daytrips. She'd never seen his entire show before—she'd only caught clips on the internet—so she'd convinced him to throw in a DVD of season one just to give her a taste of what he did for a living.

To say she was hooked was an understatement. One show turned into a marathon afternoon as she remained glued to the couch, watching episode after episode. He'd sat next to her, adding interesting tidbits about things that happened behind the scenes as they'd filmed the various shows, and she'd decided Andrew Shaw was the most fascinating man she'd ever met.

She also realized as the days passed that saying goodbye to him the day after tomorrow was going to suck. Big-time.

Andrew walked downstairs and came back into the room with his cell pressed to his ear. Apparently he wasn't having any luck reaching whoever he was trying to call because he sighed heavily and hung up.

His hair was wet from the shower he'd just taken. She wolf-whistled, impressed by the image of him in his trousers and collared shirt. It was a far cry from the faded jeans and t-shirts he'd been wearing on their excursions into the city.

"Well, hello, hot stuff."

He grimaced. "I hate dressing up for the dog and pony show." Andrew had informed her earlier he had a business meeting with some advertisers tonight that he couldn't miss. She assured him she'd be fine on her own for an evening.

"You look terrific. Besides, a free dinner is a free dinner."

Andrew chuckled. "Never thought of it that way. I

suppose you're right. Even so, I plan to eat and run, so I won't be back too late."

"Who were you trying to call?"

Andrew scowled. "Harper. She still won't answer the phone."

Amy grinned, well aware that her expression annoyed Andrew. He dropped down on the couch next to her and started tapping out a text. Amy leaned forward, reading as he wrote.

I know you're not at a conference, Harper. I just don't know where you are. If you don't answer my text within five minutes I'm contacting the FBI and telling them you've been abducted.

Amy rolled her eyes. "Jesus. Really? Why can't you leave the poor girl alone? She's having fun."

Andrew purposely ignored her as Amy tried to do some mental time zone math. It was five o'clock in Chicago, so Andrew was texting his sister at eight a.m.

Three minutes, Harper.

She thought maybe she should break the news to Andrew before he had a conniption over Harper's silent treatment. "Um, Andrew, you do realize your sister could still be asleep right now. It's early morning over there."

"Don't care. I know her. She sleeps with her phone right by the bed. I'm not stopping until I get her attention." Again he tapped out a text. *Two minutes, Harper.*

"If you ever tried to wake my arse up with those insane texts, I'd—"

Andrew texted again. *One minute, sis.*

"That wasn't a minute." The moment she stopped speaking, Andrew's phone dinged.

Harper's response appeared. *That was not a minute, Andrew.*

Amy laughed. "Told you so."

Andrew dismissed her taunt, his expression brightening

at Harper's reply. It occurred to Amy he really did miss his sister. She experienced a twinge of guilt for keeping him in the dark.

Ha! You are there after all. Now tell me where there is.

Amy wondered if Harper would give in.

Nope. You don't need to know. Safe. And happy. That should be all that counts.

"Goddamn it," Andrew muttered. "This is ridiculous. I don't know what the hell you two think I'm going to do."

"That's sort of the point, isn't it? Harper truly thinks you'd hop on a plane to Australia."

"I just want to talk to her." He texted once more. *If I call you, you're not going to answer, are you?*

No.

Andrew's shoulders fell. Amy felt bad. She wasn't one hundred percent sure what the dynamics were between Harper and Andrew. She knew they both adored each other, but sometimes Amy felt as if there was something else lingering beneath the surface. Neither of them had said as much, but it was there just the same.

I'm not happy about this, Harper. At least tell me where you are.

Silence met his request.

"She really is fine, Andrew."

He looked at her, then back at his silent phone. The persistent man tried again. *Are you going to tell me?*

I'm fine. Stop worrying. Be nice to Amy.

Amy smiled. "Yeah. Be nice to me."

He tossed the phone to the side. "Nice, huh?" He rose from the couch and went back into the hallway briefly. When he returned, he had something in his hands.

"What's that?"

"Your homework assignment. Tonight we're going to cover some new material." He handed her the lube and butt plug.

She narrowed her eyes. "This isn't exactly new."

"What happens after I pull the plug out will be."

Though he'd used the toy on her numerous times over the past couple of days, Andrew still hadn't fucked her arse. It sounded like that was going to change tonight.

She grinned. Lots of things were going to change. She didn't intend to stay in the house, but she wasn't about to ruin the surprise she had planned. "What do you want me to do?"

"Wait two hours and then put it in. I want your pretty ass nice and stretched out by the time I get home."

"Dirty bastard," she teased, taking the items from him. She stood and kissed him on the cheek. "I'll do my homework as long as you agree to play nice with the advertisers. You need them."

"Yes ma'am." He took her little peck on the cheek and returned it with interest, dragging his lips along her neck and teasing her earlobe with his teeth. His hands gripped her breasts and Amy could tell he was in danger of missing his dinner meeting. He was going to have to tackle rush-hour traffic.

Reluctantly, she pushed him away. "You better go now."

He sighed. "Fuck. Okay. I'll be back as soon as I can."

She laughed and pushed him toward the door. "I'll be ready for you with a surprise of my own."

He tilted his head suspiciously, but didn't bother to question her. Instead, he gave her another quick peck and left.

Amy didn't even wait until his car was out of the driveway before she sprinted upstairs.

Nearly an hour later she was back downstairs, dressed in a tight, far-too-revealing shirt she'd bought in Chicago and the leather skirt she'd packed from home. She had no idea what the standard attire was for a sex club, but she felt sexy and daring, so she was just going with it. She propped up the note she'd written for Andrew on a table in the front foyer, grabbed her small purse to stow the butt plug and lube in, then glanced out the window in time to see the cab pull up in front of the house.

Time to mark another item off the list. She wasn't sure if Andrew would be happy or angry when he arrived home to find her gone. The note was an invitation for him to join her. If he wouldn't take her to the club, she'd simply have to take herself and hope he'd follow. She didn't intend to play with anyone other than Andrew, so if he didn't come, she'd take a look around, then return home with her curiosity satisfied.

When she emerged from the taxi forty-five minutes later—idiot man got them lost twice—she stood on the sidewalk for a minute studying the inconspicuous building with a small, tastefully done sign that declared she had indeed made it to Velvet Chains. No wonder the cabbie had struggled to find it. It certainly didn't stand out in any way.

Taking a deep breath, she bolstered her courage and walked in the front door.

A man with a clipboard greeted her inside. "Name please."

Amy hadn't anticipated this. "Um, I'm Amy Wesson."

The man consulted his list. She needed to act fast, so she added, "I'm a guest of Andrew Shaw."

The man glanced up, taking in her attire. "Mr. Shaw isn't here this evening."

"I know. I'm meeting him here," she lied. Hopefully Andrew would take her up on her invitation to continue their sex play at the club. After all, they'd already initiated his bed, the shower, several floors in different rooms, the kitchen table and the couch at his house. The change of scenery would be fun.

"I'm sorry, but he doesn't appear to have called ahead to give us your name. I'll have to phone him to confirm."

She didn't want to interrupt—and potentially ruin—Andrew's business dinner. "Um. He really is expecting me."

The man nodded. "I understand. It won't take me a moment to confirm this."

She was about to tell him to forget it when there was a loud disturbance at the front entrance. The doorman's face flushed with anger and a fair amount of annoyance.

"Master Turner. I told you earlier. You can't come in here intoxicated."

The newcomer was dressed head to toe in leather, with slicked-back jet-black hair and an earring. Amy had to work hard at restraining her laughter. The guy appeared to have bought into every stereotype in terms of what a big, bad Dom should look like. He and the doorman began arguing, so Amy stepped into the shadows. When another man, the bouncer, arrived, she took the opportunity to move into the club. With any luck, the doorman would assume she left during the altercation and forget all about calling Andrew.

In the hallway she spotted a bathroom. She quickly stepped inside, grateful for a private place to calm her nerves. She walked to the sink and took in her flushed cheeks. She always blushed something fierce when she got anxious. Time to calm down. Best to lay low in here for a little while before venturing out. Just in case the doorman came looking for her.

Glancing at her purse, she grinned. Andrew had given her an order. Maybe she'd get submissive brownie points for following it. Stepping into a stall, she pulled the lube and plug out of her purse. It took her several minutes to prepare herself and the toy, to get it into place and manage to stand upright with the bloody big thing in her arse. Walking naturally was going to be a challenge.

She giggled to herself.

You're not in Oz anymore, Amy.

Returning to the sink, she washed her hands then checked her appearance in the mirror. The color in her face had faded back to normal. She touched up her eyeliner and lipstick then took one more steadying breath as she tried to bolster her courage.

She peeked out into the hallway. There was no sign of the doorman or the bouncer, so she walked toward the sound of music. Her eyes widened when she entered what appeared to be the heart of the club. It resembled a night-club, with tables and chairs scattered throughout the room, facing a stage that was set against one long wall. That was where the similarities ended.

The room was fairly dim, with most of the light provided by the stage lights that focused on a performance unlike anything Amy had ever seen. A naked man was chained to cross. He was facing away from the audience, so every person in the room had a clear view of his bare back and arse. A woman, dressed in a leather corset and skintight pants, wielded a whip. Every few seconds or so, she struck the bound man.

Amy would have been horrified if it weren't so apparent that the man loved the rough treatment, and if she hadn't recently been introduced to the concept of how pleasure and pain can indeed make strange but compelling bed partners.

She'd never anticipated how much she would like the feel of Andrew's hand as he spanked her or the tight pinch of the nipple clamps. Her American lover had wetted her whistle and she wanted to see how much more she could take and still enjoy. Hazel had always claimed Amy was her own worst enemy—possessing more curiosity than sense.

Amy didn't care. She figured life was meant to be lived and enjoyed. She refused to cower from new experiences. And this night ranked right up there as the mother of all experiences. Bloody hell.

Amy scanned the room, looking for an empty table. She didn't expect Andrew to arrive for another hour or so at least. She'd simply find a quiet area near the back, enjoy the show and start a new to-do list. As she watched the lovers at the surrounding tables, she spotted at least three or four new things she wouldn't mind trying with Andrew.

She'd just found an empty booth when a man stepped in front of her, blocking her path.

"Excuse me," she said, intending to sidestep the large man.

"Are you here alone?"

Alarm bells went off in Amy's head as she glanced up into the man's imposing face. He wasn't smiling and his eyes were cold. She'd seen jackaroos on the station who'd turned hard with the work. Men who slowly lost every bit of their humanity until they were as compassionate as a pissed-off cut snake. This man fit that mold.

"No," she said. "My date will be here soon."

"Date?"

She silently cursed herself for her stupidity. Once again, she'd let her impulsiveness overrule her intelligence, jumping into a situation she didn't understand without backup. If Marc and Keith were here, they'd read her the riot act for being such a bloody idiot.

"I'm meeting someone here."

The stranger lifted her arm, twisting it from side to side

as if looking for something. "You're not wearing a bracelet."

"So?"

"So as far as this club is concerned, you're an unattached submissive."

She frowned and glanced down at her outfit. "What makes you think I'm a submissive?"

The man snorted, the sound neither pleasant nor friendly. She had fucked up. Big-time.

"There you are," a strange voice said from behind her.

She glanced over her shoulder as a man she'd never seen before slipped his arm around her waist, pulling her back against his wide chest. Great. Now there were two big bad Doms to deal with.

"You forgot this," the man holding her said, as he lifted her arm and slid on a blue wristband. "Paulie tried to catch you at the front door, but you were too quick."

"Oh." While she was still nervous, she decided it was better to play along with the new guy than take her chances with the scary dude. At least this man had a kind smile and friendly manner.

"She's with you, Danner?"

Whoever Danner was nodded. "She's with me and Shaw. You know the deal."

Amy sucked in a relieved breath. This man knew Andrew. Maybe she was saved after all.

Mr. Nasty Guy didn't seem convinced. "Shaw's here?"

"He will be in a few minutes. Had a business meeting. If you'll excuse us, Amy and I were about to enjoy a bit of the show while we wait."

"You shouldn't walk around without the wristband." Then the jerk turned back to Danner. "I hope you and Shaw intend to see she's properly punished."

Amy opened her mouth to blast the arsehole, but Danner's arm tightened around her middle.

"It's up to Shaw and me to deal with our little sub. She isn't any of your concern, Schuster."

Schuster started to speak, then closed his mouth as his eyes landed on something behind her. Amy turned as Andrew walked up to join their little party of three.

"Is there a problem, Schuster?" Amy had never heard Andrew's voice so cold, so hard.

"Your sub was walking around without a bracelet. That's against the club rules."

Andrew smirked, unconcerned, though Amy felt guilty for causing him so much trouble. How the hell had he gotten here so fast? There was no way he could have gone home and found her note already. He was still dressed in the smart-looking shirt and trousers he wore earlier, so the doorman must've called him.

From the tension around his eyes, it didn't appear she was out of trouble yet after all. He was ticked off.

"Take it up with the owners if you're upset about it."

Schuster harrumphed. "Like that would do me any good. They're all your buddies."

"Then step off. Amy's spoken for."

Schuster shot her a dirty look and walked away from them.

Amy thought she should be relieved, but without the nasty man around, Andrew's irate look was suddenly turned on her. "What the hell do you think you're doing here?"

She shrugged. "I wanted to see the club. I told you that."

"And I said no."

Danner released her, moving to stand next to Andrew. "Why did you say no?"

Andrew took a step back. It seemed as if he'd forgotten the other man was there. "Tom, I just didn't think this was," Andrew paused awkwardly before quietly adding, "a good idea."

Tom didn't prod, didn't encourage Andrew to continue. Instead, his gaze returned to her and she noticed definite interest in his eyes. "I'm sorry, Amy. We haven't been properly introduced. I'm Tom Danner."

"You're the cameraman." Several times today, Andrew had mentioned his cameraman as they'd watched the show. She could tell from the stories Andrew told, he and Tom were very good friends.

Tom nodded. "Unfortunately, I don't have a clue who you are."

"I'm Amy Wesson, a friend of Harper's."

The answer didn't satisfy Tom. "The gal from Australia?"

Andrew looked at Tom. "You remembered her name?"

Tom shook his head, laugh lines crinkling around his eyes. "Jesus, buddy. You have the attention span of a three-year-old sometimes. You're the pen pal friend, right?"

Amy was impressed. "Yep, Harper and I started out chatting online about the pen pal program, but then one thing led to another and we decided to do a life swap for a couple weeks."

Tom turned to Andrew. "Harper's in Australia?"

Andrew grimaced. "Yeah."

Shock permeated Tom's features. "And you're not there? Shadowing her every move?"

Amy gave Andrew an *I told you so* look that seemed to add to his annoyance. If she were even remotely intelligent, she wouldn't poke the bear. But excessive cleverness wasn't something she'd ever been accused of.

"I don't know exactly where she is in Australia."

Tom looked from Andrew to Amy then a grin split his face. "You won't tell him."

It wasn't a question, but Amy answered anyway. "She's perfectly safe. If I thought she needed rescuing I'd tell him where to find her."

Tom released a brief, loud bark of laughter. Amy decided then and there she liked the cameraman. "None of this explains why *you're* here. And why you refused to bring her to begin with, Andrew. Guests are always welcome at parties as long as they're accompanied by a member."

"I wanted to surprise you," Amy said to Andrew. "I left you a note at home."

"I never made it home. Paulie phoned to chastise me for forgetting to call and leave the name of my guest."

She gave him an embarrassed smile, regret crinkling her nose. "Sorry. Did I mess up your deal with the advertisers?"

"Dinner was nearly over, so it was no problem for me to claim I had an emergency to attend to."

"Well, that's good, I guess. I'm glad you're here."

Andrew took her hand in his, lifting it to his lips to kiss. It was an old-fashioned gesture, but he still managed to make it feel like pure seduction as he opened his mouth, taking one of her fingers inside to suck on it.

Tom's eyes widened. "Looks like you two have become friendly as well."

Amy flashed Tom a smile. "Andrew's teaching me how to be a submissive."

Tom choked. "Damn. You're doing a helluva job so far, Shaw."

Andrew narrowed his gaze, giving Tom a dirty look. "Fuck you. I told you to stay home, Amy."

"I thought it might be more fun to move our lessons here."

"Yeah, well, lucky for you, Tom was already here and able to intervene. Otherwise, you'd most likely be spending the evening with Schuster."

"The arsehole? No way."

Tom explained. "Amy, you walked into the social room without a Dom or a bracelet. That's an open invitation."

"And I don't get any say-so?"

Tom shook his head. "Not tonight. It's a *private* party and there are some fairly strict rules regarding the play at this one."

She bit her lip. "Oh. Sorry again. I didn't realize."

Tom shrugged good-naturedly. "No harm, no foul. So…are you two planning to stick around for a while?"

Andrew didn't respond immediately. Instead he studied his friend's face before looking at her. His expression was less angry now. If anything, he seemed to be uptight. Then he nodded slowly. "Sure. Why not? We're already here."

Just when Amy didn't think Tom's grin could get any bigger, he proved her wrong. "Awesome." He reached into his pocket for something. "I reserved room seven when I checked in."

Andrew looked at him. "I told you I wasn't coming."

Tom lifted his shoulder. "I was horny tonight. Planning my first solo act."

Amy tried to follow their conversation, but wasn't having much luck. For a second, it almost sounded as if Andrew and Tom were a couple. "Um, should I leave?"

Tom laughed again. "Hell no. This party doesn't happen without you."

"What party?"

Andrew closed his eyes briefly. "Come on, Amy. We're

going to deal with your misbehavior. Then we're going to continue those lessons."

"We?"

"Yeah. Tom and I."

Amy's mouth went dry as she tried to process Andrew's answer. "Um…"

His face lost its tension, as it appeared he'd made up his mind. "You know your safe word. If you want to say it, say it." She tried to decide if he was hoping for that very occurrence. She didn't think so, but she couldn't tell for sure.

Then he winked at her.

Bloody hell. She'd been sleeping with Andrew Shaw for exactly four nights and already the man knew her biggest weaknesses. Her pride wouldn't let her back down from what felt like a blatant dare and she'd already tested the safe word. She knew he would keep his promise and stop. If she said no to this experience, she'd regret it for the rest of her life.

She'd told Harper her sexual fantasy was to sleep with a stranger. Now Andrew was offering her another chance to explore that kink.

She studied Tom's face. He would walk away if she spoke the word, she could see it in his eyes. She could also read the hope that lingered there as well.

"I'm not going to say the word."

Tom released a long breath. "Thank God. After you." He allowed Andrew, who still held her hand, to lead her out of the social room and down a dimly lit, but elegantly decorated corridor. They stopped in front of a room and Tom held up a keycard, like those used in hotels. For a sex club, Velvet Chains was certainly more upscale and classy than she'd expected.

The three of them stepped into the room together. It was a stylish space, well lit with over a dozen candles.

"Wow."

Andrew squeezed her hand. She hadn't faced him since agreeing to the ménage. Part of her was afraid of what she'd see. Did he want this? He'd been the one to suggest it, but there was something in his eyes that had appeared hesitant, uncertain.

She forced her gaze to meet his and breathed a sigh of relief. Andrew was the same, his face compassionate, patient, understanding.

"I have a suspicion this isn't exactly uncharted territory for you guys."

Andrew shook his head. "No. It's not new to us. We always share at the club."

"Always?"

He hesitated long enough to let her know this wasn't a conversation he was comfortable having. She'd noticed the same reticence when he'd talked about his family. Andrew Shaw was a private man, which made her all the more interested in peeling back the layers. She wanted to know more about him. Everything.

Which was a bad plan. He was returning to work in two days and she was going home to Farpoint a week later. Better to keep things casual. Fun sex with no strings. Anything more than that was going to be dangerous to her heart.

"Andrew was the one who introduced me to the club, to BDSM. I was anxious to learn more about domination and submission. He offered to walk me through the paces the first few times, but it soon became apparent we liked sharing women. Since then, whenever we're at the club, we share."

Tom's explanation sparked more questions in Amy's

mind. Was that why Andrew had refused to bring her to the club? Because he knew the evening would end with Tom in their bed? If that was true and he didn't want it, then why were they all in this room together now?

"You only share at the club?"

Andrew nodded. "We've limited the threesome play to here. We don't indulge in the same games when we're on the road."

"Or whenever you're in a serious relationship with a woman?" She was digging. Amy hoped Andrew didn't figure it out.

Tom chuckled. "I don't share my girlfriends with Andrew."

The answer didn't satisfy her. Didn't tell her what she wanted to know.

When Andrew failed to respond, Tom filled in the other blank. "And Shaw here is a commitment-phobe. Never been in a serious relationship with a woman in all the time I've known him."

Tom missed the slight wince his words provoked from Andrew, but Amy didn't. She wasn't sure how to handle that information. Not that it mattered. She couldn't be his girlfriend. Time and geography were not on her side. But she couldn't help wondering why Andrew was reluctant to fall in love, to get close to someone. From all Harper had said over the past year, she knew Andrew loved his sister intensely. So why was he resistant to letting those emotions carry over to someone else?

Andrew stepped closer, pulling her shirt over her head before she could consider his actions or the consequences of them. It was an evasion—pure and simple. The conversation was over.

It didn't matter. She was ready for this.

Her heart skipped a beat when Tom came up behind

her, his hands gripping her bare waist, his lips lightly kissing the side of her neck.

Andrew watched her, studied her reactions. She smiled as she ran her hand along his chest. Slipping loose the buttons on his shirt, Andrew pulled it off so she could touch bare skin.

Tom unfastened her bra, letting the lace fall to the floor. Amy shivered slightly when he reached around her, touching her breasts, toying with her tight nipples.

"God," she said on a hushed breath.

Andrew smiled. "You're so fucking sexy, Amy."

She lifted her hands to his shoulders. "Kiss me."

Andrew complied, bending to press his lips against hers as Tom continued to play with her breasts. Andrew cupped her cheeks in his large, strong palms, turning her head to deepen the kiss. She'd never tasted such passion. For a moment, she actually felt lightheaded.

Tom's hands drift lower, moving to the back once more as his fingers worked to lower the zipper on her leather skirt. Then he tugged the tight material over her hips. Amy kicked it off when it hit the floor. She was completely naked except for her G-string and heels.

Tom's hands ran over her bare buttocks. When his fingers traced the thin strap of her G-string along her slit and discovering her secret, he groaned. "Jesus, Andrew. What the fuck?"

His amazed tone distracted Andrew, who released her lips. She winked at him and he grinned. "So basically you only followed one of my instructions for tonight."

She shrugged. "Yep. But I figured it was the one that really mattered."

Tom stopped touching her, so she glanced over her shoulder. He was giving Andrew an odd look. "She disobeyed you by coming here. Should we punish her?"

Andrew shook his head quickly. "No. I'll take care of the punishment later."

Tom frowned. "But—"

"I said I'd handle it, Tom."

Confusion filled Tom's eyes, but he dropped the subject. "Why don't we move this party to the bed?"

Amy swallowed heavily. Bloody hell. She was really going to do this, wasn't she? She kept waiting for panic to set in, but her damn libido had kicked that emotion to the curb. She led the way to the bed, soaking up the sound of both men chuckling behind her.

"Anxious, Amy?" Andrew asked.

She threw him a sexy grin over her shoulder. "Very. So hurry up."

Tom scowled but Andrew didn't take offense at her haughty demand. Instead, he walked over and placed a none-too-gentle smack on her arse. "Behave, wildcat."

She closed her eyes, trying to think of something else saucy to say to get him to spank the other cheek.

Before she could come up with a witty reply, Andrew's hand pressed on her shoulder. "Bend over. Let's get that plug out of you, so we can fill you up with something a bit warmer. Like me."

She let Andrew push her forward until her elbows hit the mattress. Then he tapped on her inner ankles, indicating he wanted her to spread her legs. She complied as both men stepped behind her. Her body grew warm as she considered exactly what she was displaying.

"God fucking dammit," Tom muttered. "What an ass."

She giggled, the sound provoked by equal portions of nerves and delight. She'd never felt sexy back home. She'd grown up with most of the available men on the station. As a result, they didn't seem able to look beyond the little girl she'd been to notice the woman she'd become.

Andrew's hand stroked her arse before pulling her G-string aside and grasping the end of the plug. He slowly pulled it out as Amy fought not to squirm with pleasure. He was going to take her there. She sucked in a deep breath, trying to calm down, her patience ebbing. She wanted him now.

A *thunk* behind her told her Andrew had dropped the plug to the floor. Maybe she wasn't the only one struggling to go slowly.

"Get undressed and get on the bed, Tom. On your back." As Andrew directed the other man, Andrew helped her stand with a steadying hand on her arm. Tom began to disrobe and Amy became aware of who the more dominant Dom in the room was. Andrew was going to call the shots and, given Tom's quick response, he would be obeyed.

At least by Tom.

She tried not to laugh at the thought.

"That's not a look I trust," Andrew whispered, noticing her humor.

"That's because you're smart." She turned her attention back to Tom as her mirth dissipated. Bloody hell. The cameraman was built. His clothing had been too baggy to fully display the muscles the man was packing. He'd be hell on the rugby field.

Once Tom was naked, he lay down on the mattress, his hard cock betraying his own enthusiasm for their play.

"Now you." Andrew tugged her G-string down. "Kick off your shoes."

She toed off the heels, instantly missing the three extra inches of height. Andrew suddenly loomed over her again. While she liked feeling petite next to him, there was definitely some power in being taller.

Andrew kissed the top of her head. "Crawl onto the bed. Get on your hands and knees, over Tom's body."

She reacted quickly, not giving herself time to consider her compliance. Tom reached for her breasts as she climbed over him, his palms cupping the fleshy mounds.

"You're beautiful, Amy."

Tom's kind words washed away the last trace of doubt. Tonight would be yet another memory of the greatest trip of her life. Another image she could pull out to dream about when life at Farpoint became routine, dreary or unbearable.

The mattress sank as Andrew joined them. It was only then that Amy realized he'd shed his clothing as well. His hand stroked her arse.

"Amy—" he started.

"I'm not saying the word, Andrew. Promise." She cut him off, knowing he was offering her one more out. She wasn't taking it. If she walked away from these men and their sexy, amazing offer now, she'd regret it for the rest of her life. She wasn't interested in regrets.

Andrew reached toward the nightstand, retrieving a new tube of lubrication and two condoms. "You can still say the word, Amy. Anytime. Just remember that."

She nodded, then gasped when he pressed the nozzle of the lube into her arse and squeezed. She was still slick from the lubrication she'd used on the plug, but she appreciated Andrew's thoughtfulness. She was new to this and he was going out of his way to make sure she didn't experience too much pain.

He worked the sticky gel inside her with one finger, and then two. The pressure felt good, made her hot. She pushed against his thrusts, trying to drive him deeper. His free hand gripped her hip firmly. "Don't move, Amy. I know you don't like to take orders, but you will obey me on this. We're doing this at my pace. Not yours. If you can't follow that command, I'll turn you over my knee until you understand exactly who's in charge here."

Bloody hell. Andrew's deep tone, his darkly sensual threat sent shivers through her body. Maybe she was more submissive than she realized because at that moment, she suspected she'd kiss his feet if he demanded she do so.

"Yes Sir," she whispered.

Tom grinned at her reply, his expression one of surprise and humor. He seemed to understand the words didn't come naturally to her, but he clearly appreciated her attempt. "Come here, Amy."

Tom's hands engulfed her waist, pulling her down until the head of his cock nudged at her entrance.

"Forgetting something, Danner?"

Tom grimaced. "Fuck. Yeah." He held his hand out as Andrew dropped a condom into it. Amy giggled when he tore the package open with his teeth then donned the thing in record time.

"Get back here." Tom pulled her in place over his cock. As he guided her hips, she slowly lowered herself onto his wide girth. He wasn't quite as large as Andrew, but he had enough to hit her hot spots.

Amy gasped. She was having sex with a stranger. Again.

Once Tom was fully seated, his grip tightened and he held her still. She started to protest his firm hold, wanting more friction, more movement, but Andrew's hand caressed her arse and she froze.

Moment of truth.

She heard the second condom wrapper open mere seconds before she felt Andrew's cock nudging at the tight opening of her anus. She closed her eyes and held her breath.

"Breathe," Tom coaxed. "And try to relax."

Easier said than done. Andrew was much larger than the plug. Stretched arsehole or not, this was going to hurt.

"Okay, Amy?" Andrew asked.

The compassion in his voice instantly relaxed her. This was Andrew. He would take care of her. She let the magic of the moment sweep her away. "Yes."

Andrew slowly pressed in, stopping several times to give her a chance to adjust, to accept this new erotic invasion.

Finally, the last inch found its way home. None of them moved. Instead, they savored the sensations of being so closely connected—bound by flesh and sweat and passion.

Andrew was the first to break the silence. "Jesus," he muttered. "Amy."

Her heart beat faster at the sound of her name, spoken in hushed tones. Bloody hell, she'd never felt so cherished, so adored. This was bad. Just a few days in and she was falling hard for Andrew Shaw. Really hard.

Tom began to thrust his hips, the shallow movement rocking her to the core. "Holy God," she whispered.

Tom stopped.

She shook her head. "No. Keep going. Please."

Andrew's hand caressed her arse gently, then he gripped her hips and took her at her word. She'd never experienced anything so intense or overwhelming. Every sense in her body was on full alert as tingles raced along her spine. Both men murmured sexy words as they stroked her sensitive skin. Sweat rolled down her cheek as the temperature in the room spiked. It felt as if she were immersed in the center of a volcano, caught in a swirling vortex of heat, pain, pleasure.

Tom cupped her breasts, kneading her heavy flesh as Andrew grasped her hips, using his hands to drive her motions. And his. And Tom's. He was in control of them all, directing the symphony until thunder roared in her ears and she screamed out her release.

Tom followed her next, his deep voice groaning as he came inside her. Andrew was the last to be consumed. He leaned over her back, kissing her shoulder and the nape of her neck as he whispered her name, again and again.

"Bloody hell," she said at last as both men chucked exhaustedly.

Andrew pulled out carefully, then collapsed onto the mattress by their side. She lay boneless atop Tom's body, unable to move. They were all breathing heavily, Tom's heart beating out a rapid rhythm in her ear.

Amy's eyes drifted open, closed, then open again. She was sluggish, replete, exhausted.

Tom's hand cupped her jaw and he lifted her face. "You were incredible, Amy."

She froze when she realized he was leaning closer to kiss her. It was silly to hesitate, considering his flaccid penis was still inside her. Regardless, it was Andrew's kisses she craved.

Tom was a mere inch from her when Andrew's deep voice cut the silence. "Wait."

Tom paused, glancing over at Andrew.

Slowly, Andrew sat up and reached for her. She pushed herself up as well.

"Come here, Amy," Andrew beckoned.

She let him take her into his arms, wrapping her tight in his powerful embrace. "Thank you for keeping an eye on her until I could get here, Tom."

Tom's gaze narrowed. "That sounds like a dismissal."

Andrew lifted one shoulder. Amy watched the two friends with fascination, listening to the words that weren't being spoken. Andrew didn't want Tom to kiss her. She tried not to let that idea sink in too deeply. She was already having trouble with her heart. This romantic gesture wasn't going to help.

"I'm sorry. I just…" Andrew's words faded, but neither she nor Tom needed to hear the rest.

Tom grinned. "Gotcha." He placed a soft kiss on Amy's cheek. "Thanks for a wonderful evening."

She laughed. Talk about an understatement. She'd never had a night like this and couldn't for the life of her figure out a way she could ever top it. "Ta muchly, Tom."

He dressed, his gaze returning to the two of them sitting in each other's arms. Andrew hadn't moved to kiss her or cover her up. In fact, the poor lad was looking a bit shell-shocked. It was awesome.

As Tom walked to the door, he turned and gave them a quick nod. Then he said, "It's about time," and left.

Andrew released a long breath. She wanted to call him out, to question why he'd sent Tom away. She didn't get a chance.

Andrew told her everything she needed to know with his kiss. He gripped her cheeks between his hands, placed his lips on hers and the world brightened with crystal-clear focus.

Her bloody heart gave up the fight. It surrendered a very large part to Andrew Shaw and it was pointless to try to hold on to it.

Chapter Six

ndrew heard the mail fall through the slot in the front door. Rising from the couch, he walked to the foyer to retrieve it. Amy stretched out on the cushions, looking relaxed, happy. Last night's trip to Velvet Chains had opened his eyes to some fairly hard truths.

While he didn't mind sharing Amy with Tom, he'd never repeat the experience. In the past, he'd preferred the threesomes of the club, allowing Tom to do the lion's share of coddling and cuddling as he directed the sex play. Tom had handled the emotional side of sex, complimenting their partners, putting them at ease with friendly comment and kisses.

Andrew had never taken that role, happy to remain detached while getting his rocks off. Last night, the roles had been reversed. He had seen the look of surprise on Tom's face when Andrew pulled Amy away from him. Tom would no doubt be calling at some point to question him at length about who exactly Amy was and what she meant to him.

Problem was Andrew didn't have any goddamn

answers. Not a single fucking one. His heart was engaged, but it didn't matter. He'd received an email that morning, informing him of a meeting in Los Angeles he'd have to attend the following afternoon. He was going back to work and Amy was going home next week. So that was it. Game over. End of story.

Bending over, he picked up the mail, flipping through the junk and bills. Then he spotted a plain white envelope with just Amy's name on it, written in Harper's handwriting. Curious, Andrew opened the door and glanced down the street, wondering where the letter had come from. He spotted Mrs. Haskiell, the elderly lady across the street, walking back into her house. Harper often looked in on the older lady, who had recently been widowed. Had she delivered the letter?

He dumped the rest of the mail in the basket by the door and carried Amy's letter back to the living room.

"There's something here for you. From Harper."

Amy brightened and sat up. "For me? Really? Cool." She took the envelope, tore it open and pulled out what appeared to be two tickets. Then she started laughing.

"What is it?"

Amy flashed the baseball tickets at him. "I think this is my surprise from Harper. We got into a fight once over which sport was better—cricket or baseball. Apparently your sister decided I need to experience the sport firsthand in order to make an educated decision."

Andrew grinned as he recalled the final two texts he'd sent to Harper last night. He'd been bored out of his mind at dinner with the advertisers and thinking nonstop about his lovely Aussie houseguest. Without Harper's uncharacteristic impulsiveness, he never would have met Amy, so he'd thrown a dog a bone and written Harper back, giving in—as much as he could. *Fine. Have it your way. I won't keep hassling you about where you are. But I won't stop worrying. I can't. It's what I do, right?*

He was annoyed as hell at Harper for taking off without telling him, but he had to appreciate the fact she'd brought Amy into his life. Even so, he'd decided to tweak his sister and get a bit of revenge, so he'd texted her one last line. *Just remember when you get home, YOU told me to be nice to Amy.*

Harper could make what she wanted of that. Then his brain engaged and he frowned. "She sent you two tickets?"

Amy nodded. "Weird, right? I'll have to text her to see if she had someone specific in mind for me to go with. Maybe she's setting me up on a blind date."

Andrew scowled. "Doesn't matter if she is. You're going to that game with me."

"Maybe. Maybe not. They're my tickets. I can go with anybody I want to."

He tugged on her ankle, pulling her beneath him on the couch, enjoying her teasing. "Give me the ticket, Amy."

"What will you give me in return?"

"What do you want?" At that moment, there was very little he wouldn't offer his sexy little Aussie.

"Another lesson? More drilling?"

He laughed. "Drilling sounds good." He leaned closer and kissed her. He'd never been much for kissing, but there was something irresistible about Amy's lips, the way she played with the hair at the nape of his neck and her quiet murmurs. She approached the act the way she did most things—she dove in headfirst with boundless enthusiasm and energy.

She was a breath of fresh air after months of sucking in nothing but pollution. It was going to be hell saying goodbye to her tomorrow.

He pushed the thought away. They still had today and he was going to make it count.

Amy lifted her legs and wrapped them around his waist, pressing her pussy against his erection. Both of them had donned lightweight sweatpants and t-shirts this morning. Going for comfort as they'd elected to enjoy a lazy day at home.

Now it looked like they were going to spend the afternoon at a ballgame. As much as he'd love to drag out this sexual escapade, they'd have to settle for a quickie with the promise of more, later tonight.

"You sore?" He was concerned about her after their adventure in the club. Neither he nor Tom had held back, both of them losing themselves inside Amy's sweet body.

She shook her head. "I feel incredible. Last night was…" She paused and he wondered what word she would use to describe it. "It was bloody amazing."

"So you think you might give the threesome thing a try again?"

"No." Her response was quick and took him by surprise.

"Why not?" Had he misread her? He thought she'd enjoyed the experience.

"Because I don't think you want to do it again and, honestly, you're the only person I can picture myself ever doing that with."

He'd given himself away to more than just Tom. Amy had picked up on his unease over sharing her as well. "I'm sorry, Amy. I don't want you to think I didn't love what we did at the club, I—"

"Oh, I know you did. I loved it as well. But, well, I like it better when it's just us. If that makes sense."

It made perfect sense. He felt exactly the same way. He rose from the couch and pulled his pants down. His erection stood out long and hard. Amy sat up in front of him, grasping it in her hand.

He cupped the sides of her face and tilted until she looked at him. "I want you to suck my cock."

She gave him a saucy smile. "I thought you'd never ask."

Without a moment's hesitation, she engulfed the head with her sweet lips. He didn't bother to restrain his groan of absolute bliss when she took him deep on the first pass. Her mouth was lethal to his control as she used her tongue and teeth to tease his sensitive flesh.

"God, Amy. That feels so fucking good."

She increased her pace and the pressure, taking him from zero to sixty in less than a minute. Damn. He wanted this to last, but she wasn't holding anything back. It had been this way since their first night together. Amy gave herself over to him, without reservation. She didn't seem to suffer the same misgivings as other lovers he'd been with in the past. Instead, she was simply herself.

One of her hands tightened at the base of his dick and Andrew saw stars. When she used her free hand to up the ante, stroking her fingers between his ass cheeks, toying with his anus, he knew he was a goner.

"Shit. Amy. I'm not going to be able to stop."

She wiggled her finger harder against his tight opening, pressing in to the first knuckle.

Game over. Once again, she'd come out on top.

His fingers tightened in her dark tresses. He loved the soft texture of her hair. Amy showed no mercy as she continued to suck on his cock.

When he came, she swallowed, then slowed her sucking.

He gasped for breath, his heart galloping a million

miles a minute. He'd spent nearly a week inside her, and yet every experience was as exciting as the first.

Amy released him with a pop. Her too-pleased grin proved she knew exactly what effect she had on him.

"Come on." He grasped her hand and pulled her up.

"Where are we going?"

"Shower. I need a few minutes to recover."

She stood to follow, but her cell phone rang. Amy bent to retrieve it from the coffee table and glanced at the screen. She grinned. "It's Harper. She's probably checking to make sure I got the tickets."

Andrew held out his hand, indicating he wanted the phone.

Amy shook her head. "Nope. She called me. Not you. Go start the shower. I'll be there in a minute."

He wanted to protest, but he knew if Harper were in trouble, Amy wouldn't hesitate to tell him. Best to let them have their girl time.

"Tell her I said hello. And that we're going to have a long chat when she gets back home."

Amy laughed. "Big bully." Then she clicked on the phone and said, "Hello."

He picked up his sweatpants and headed upstairs.

"WHAT'S UP, GIRLFRIEND?" Amy said. "It's kind of late for you to be up, isn't it? Tomorrow's a school day."

"I just wanted to hear a friendly voice."

Harper's tone set off alarm bells in Amy's head. "What's wrong?"

Silence met her question until Amy prompted again, "Harper?"

"I had a bad day. I fucked up."

Amy couldn't imagine anything Harper could do that would be so bad. "In class?"

"Oh no. The kids are awesome. Seriously. I love them. It's something more…personal."

"You're going to have to give me more to go on, Harper."

Again, her friend didn't immediately reply. Like sister, like brother. The similarities between Andrew and Harper were never more apparent. Both of them played their cards close to their chests.

"Listen. If you can't talk to me, what about Marc or Keith? I'm sure either one of them—"

She didn't have a chance to finish her comment before the sound of Harper crying cut her off.

"Holy crap. You're killing me. Please don't cry. What's wrong?"

"Marc and Keith are wonderful. But I screwed things up with them. And then Ronnie…" Harper's words faded away and Amy sensed she was struggling to pull herself together.

"Ronnie? You mean Big Mac? That guy's an arsehole. If he's bothering you, tell Keith, or hell, if you can't do that, tell Hunter or Hazel. Don't let him hassle you."

"How's Andrew?"

It was an abrupt change of topic and it took Amy a second to switch gears.

"He's fine."

"I miss him."

Amy wanted to chalk the phone call up to homesickness, but it was clear there was something else at work. "He misses you too. Do you want to talk to him? He's just upstairs. I can—"

"No! No, please don't tell him that I'm crying. He'll flip

out. I don't want to cause him any more worry. I've hurt him enough."

What the fuck did that mean? "If you're upset or hurt, Andrew would want to know. I've kept the fact you're at Farpoint a secret because I thought you were safe and happy. It doesn't sound like that's true anymore. What do you want? Do you need me to fly home? Or do you want to come back to Chicago?"

Harper sighed. "I don't want to come home."

Amy wasn't sure what comfort she could offer. She felt helpless, too far away. "Tell me what you need, Harper. I hate that you're sad."

Harper scoffed, the sound filled with sadness. "I thought I'd kicked the demons of my past to the curb. These last few days have been perfect, some of the best of my life. I got blindsided today and now I'm struggling to find my way back."

"Demons?"

"One day I'll tell you about why I came to live with Andrew and my dad when I was a kid. For now, let's just leave it at my stepdad wasn't a very nice person."

Amy's heart lurched. Had Harper been abused? That would definitely explain Andrew's tendency to be overprotective of his sister and her hesitance to put herself out there, to take chances. "We're going to have that talk."

"I know. I want to tell you. I need to tell someone. I can't talk to Andrew because he feels guilty about it. Listen. I'm sorry I called. I can tell you're having a great time and I really didn't mean to bring you down or ruin your trip. I'm just having a pity party tonight. I'm sure things will be better in the morning."

Harper's tone didn't match her words. Amy couldn't help but think the morning wasn't going to be much better for her friend. Had she inadvertently unearthed some best-buried can of worms with this damn life-swap idea?

"If they aren't, call me. Or text. I'm sure we can figure this out. Somehow."

"Okay. Give Andrew my love."

Amy felt sick to her stomach. "Sure."

"Goodbye, Amy."

"See you later." Amy tapped End on her iPhone and tried to figure out what the hell she was supposed to do now. Harper had asked her not to tell Andrew she was upset, but this secret wasn't sitting as easily on her shoulders.

THE PHONE CONVERSATION returned to her at various times during the day. She'd tried to concentrate on the baseball game, to let herself enjoy the moment and Andrew's hilarious, over-the-top, maniac-like devotion to his Sox, but she couldn't shake her worrying.

All day long she kept asking herself what Andrew would say if something truly bad had happened to Harper at Farpoint and he discovered Amy hadn't told him.

He'd never forgive her. Bloody hell, she'd never forgive herself.

"Earth to Amy."

She blinked a couple times, letting her vision focus on Andrew once more. They'd returned home from the game an hour ago. Andrew had offered to make her dinner at home, as neither of them wanted to spend their last night together in some crowded restaurant. They'd eaten most of the meal in silence.

It was the end. Amy's chest tightened. They would say goodbye tomorrow morning, most likely forever. "Sorry."

"What's going on, Amy? You've been lost in the Twilight Zone most of the day."

"I'm worried about Harper." She hadn't meant to blurt it out so abruptly, but something told her Andrew needed to know what was going on. Maybe he could shed some light on the demons Harper alluded to, so Amy would know if she needed to call Keith.

Several times today she'd considered texting him to see what the hell was going on, but something held her back.

Andrew scowled. "Why?"

"She was a little upset this morning when she called."

She'd never seen such a dark expression on Andrew's face. Not even during his confrontation with Schuster at the club the previous night. "What the fuck did she say? What happened?"

Andrew rose from the dinner table, pacing to the counter. He slapped his hand on the smooth surface and she jumped. "Goddamn it. You swore to me she was safe. That she was happy."

"She is. Or was. I don't know what happened. She wouldn't say."

Andrew stopped listening. He pulled his cell out of his pocket and dialed. No doubt he was calling his sister. Amy's gut told him she wouldn't answer.

Pure anger radiated when he spoke. She'd been right. He'd gotten Harper's voice mail. "Call me. Now."

He slammed the phone down and started pacing. Amy wasn't sure what to say to calm him. His response seemed so over-the-top.

Amy was too tired to even try to figure out what time it was on the other side of the planet. Most likely Harper was teaching class and didn't have her phone turned on.

"What happened between Harper and her stepdad?"

she asked after several minutes proved his sister wasn't going to return his call.

Andrew froze, his gaze capturing hers. "She told you?"

Amy shook her head. "Nothing in detail. She just said he wasn't a nice man."

Andrew snorted, the sound malicious, cold. "That's a fucking understatement."

"He hurt her?"

Andrew's chest rose and fell, his breathing coming harder now. She'd never seen him out of control. Her dominant lover never lost his cool. He didn't speak and the silence grew unbearably long.

"I'm sorry," she said softly. "I shouldn't have pried. Shouldn't have agreed to this life swap. I didn't know…"

What? She didn't know what?

"It's okay, Amy. Harper needs someone like you in her life. God knows you're probably better for her than I am."

She shook her head, hating the sudden desolation in his eyes. "No. You're wrong. Your sister loves you."

"I have no idea why. She should hate me."

Amy frowned. "Why? Why would you say that?"

"Because I left her alone with that man. She called me and asked for help and I brushed her off."

Amy walked to him and took his hands, led him back to the table, to his chair. "Sit down. Start at the beginning."

He followed her command, his head bent. Amy's heart ached for him.

"I've never told anyone about this. I was too…" He paused. "I was too fucking ashamed of myself."

She returned to her own chair then clasped his hands in hers. "Tell me."

"Remember how I said Harper went to live with her mother after our parents divorced?"

She nodded.

"Her mom remarried pretty soon after that. The guy, Ross, was a slimeball. Harper hated him almost instantly, but I figured she was at that age where she resented having a new father. After all, I'd had those same feelings when my dad married her mom."

"That makes sense. She must've been what? Eleven, twelve?"

"Ten. Anyway, Harper lived with them for nearly a year. She sort of started withdrawing, getting quieter, more sullen. Like a dumbass, I chalked it all up to early puberty."

Amy gave him a sympathetic smile. "That's a rational assumption."

Andrew's grip on her hand tightened. She sensed he was trying to draw strength from her. She was happy to give it. "I was wrong. She called me one night. I'd just turned twenty-one a few months earlier and I was enjoying the newfound privileges, getting ripped with my friends every weekend. I'd planned to do some serious club-hopping that night. Harper asked if I would come get her. If she could spend the weekend with me and Dad."

Andrew swallowed heavily and Amy suspected this was where the story would get tougher. She gave him an encouraging smile.

"I guess you said no."

He nodded.

"You were young with fun plans. I don't think there's an older brother on the planet who would have given those up willingly just so he could babysit his kid sister. Where was your dad?"

"He was out of town on a business trip. I should have gone to get her right then. I could hear in her voice she was scared. She said her mom was out for the night and she didn't like to be alone with Ross. I told her to just go to her room and watch TV."

He closed his eyes, but not before she caught the flash of pain there.

"I went out, hit a couple of clubs, but I couldn't shake the idea that something was wrong. Really wrong. I ditched my friends, grabbed a cab and headed over to check on Harper. No one answered the door when I got there, but I could see Ross' car in the driveway. Then I heard Harper call out."

Amy tried not to cry. Her tears wouldn't help Andrew, but his story was tearing her apart. "What did you do?"

"I kicked the door down."

Jesus. She'd seen snatches of his incredible strength over the past few days, but she could only imagine the force he'd produced to break down a door.

"I ran down the hall to Harper's room just as Ross was rushing out. The son of a bitch was zipping up his pants."

"Bloody hell," Amy whispered. "Did he…had he…?"

"No. I got there before he could…" Andrew took a deep breath, steadying himself before he was able to say, "Rape her."

Amy closed her eyes. "Thank God."

"I punched the motherfucker hard enough to knock him out. Then I grabbed a suitcase and started shoving a bunch of shit in it. I picked Harper up and I carried her out of there."

Amy couldn't stand the distance between them any longer or the pain etched on every line in his face. She left her chair and knelt before him. "You saved her, Andrew. Where's the shame in that?"

"I should have gone when she called. Should have taken her away from there before it got that far. I let her down, Amy. I didn't protect her."

Andrew was a strong, proud man. Those attributes had likely been there since birth. She couldn't imagine how many nights he'd suffered, thinking of how he'd failed his sister. The pain he carried for so many years must have been unbearable.

"You're a good man, Andrew. You took your sister out of hell. You brought her here and provided a safe, loving home. Even when your dad passed away, you stuck around and raised her. You're amazing. Loving. Wonderful."

He started to shake his head, but she refused to let him deny the truth. "Bloody hell, Shaw. Stop beating yourself up over this. It's time to let the past go. You and Harper are both alive, healthy, together. Start facing forward, looking toward your future. The past can't hurt either of you anymore. Besides, Harper clearly doesn't blame you."

"How do you know?"

"I know because she misses you. She may have called *me* this morning, but I guarantee it was your voice she really needed to hear."

He gestured to his cell. "Yeah. I can tell. She ran off to Australia without telling me and she's been ringing my phone off the hook since then."

"She's in class right now."

He frowned. "Class?"

Amy nodded. "She's teaching my students at Farpoint Creek Cattle Station. It's just outside Cobar."

Andrew's eyes softened, though the sadness still lingered. "You really are a cowgirl, living on a ranch."

She laughed. "No. I live on a station and there's no cowgirl about it."

"Come to bed with me?" His request was hesitant, uncertain. Spoken by a broken man.

She smiled and kissed him on the cheek. "There's nowhere on earth I'd rather be."

They held hands as they climbed the stairs together. Kissing, they took turns slowly undressing each other. Neither of them seemed inclined to stop touching, to break the connection.

He lifted her, placing her gently on the mattress before crawling over her body. She loved being sheltered beneath his large, strong form. Andrew continued to kiss her as he pressed his cock inside, the path a familiar one to him now. He understood where to press, appreciated how fast, how hard she liked it. He knew her body.

He knew *her*.

And now, she felt like she knew him. It made the moment so much more precious. And painful.

She wrapped her arms around his shoulders, holding him to her tightly as they rocked together. Time stood still as they clung to each other. For so many years, she'd felt lost, just a little out of step with everyone else around her.

With Andrew, she was the true Amy. It was a precious gift he offered.

When they came, it was together. Bittersweet and beautiful as the clock continued to count down.

Tomorrow he'd say goodbye. Fly away on other adventures, traveling off the beaten paths, while she returned to one that was way too familiar in Australia.

Funny how Farpoint didn't feel like home anymore.

She wondered if it ever would again.

Chapter Seven

Amy looked at the blue mountains in the distance and knew she'd come home. After a tearful farewell to Andrew in Chicago two days earlier, it had taken her all of five minutes to decide she wanted to return to Farpoint. America held no fascination for her without him in it.

She sniffed the light scent of eucalyptus from the gum trees and remembered Andrew's complaint about the way her country smelled like medicine. Now she wasn't sure she could ever inhale the faint odor without thinking of him.

She was home. Back in the land of brown eggs covered in feathers and poo, spiders on the loo, no tipping and super-short showers that turned cold too quickly.

As much as she'd wanted to escape Chicago and its memories of Andrew, Farpoint didn't seem very welcoming either. Bloody hell. What had she done? Lived a lifetime in ignorant bliss, moving from moment to moment without a care in the world. In one week, Andrew had made her care too much. About him.

Surely this feeling would fade with time.

Wouldn't it?

She hoped so. Right now, her heart ached and she felt like a teenage girl suffering her first lost love. She was considering holing herself up in her cottage with Harper for a week, eating ice cream from the carton and belting out one sad song after another. She was the cliché of a broken-hearted woman. Marc and Keith would have a field day with this, but she didn't give a shit.

She'd thought coming home would help. Wandering around an empty house in Chicago for a week felt too unbearable so she'd decided to come home to be with the people she loved. She also consoled herself over cutting her vacation short with the thought that, this way, she'd have a chance to hang out with Harper.

Of course, that was going to have to start after she crawled out of bed approximately three days from now. She'd never felt so exhausted. One week of sleep-deprived, sex-filled nights followed by two days on nonstop travel had zapped every ounce of energy left in her body. She suspected she could close her eyes and not open them again for days, maybe years.

Even then, she still wouldn't want to wake up. Her dreams of Andrew would have to sustain her from now on and she could only have those while asleep.

She stepped out of the ute she'd rented at the Cobar airport and was promptly greeted by Jett, Keith's black Kelpie. The dog wasn't too far ahead of his master and soon she found herself wrapped up in hugs and greetings and questions of "What the hell are you doing home already?" from her two best mates.

Only after Keith, then Marc released her, did Amy spy Harper. Her friend's familiar features and crystal blue eyes reminded her too much of the man she'd just lost. Amy took two steps and fell into Harper's embrace, tears escaping despite her best efforts to hold them at bay.

"Hey," Harper said consolingly. "Please tell me you didn't come home early because of me and that stupid phone call."

Amy shook her head. "No. Andrew…" It was all she could say before her throat seized up again.

"Oh my God. What the hell did he do? I'll kill him."

Amy laughed through her tears. "He didn't do anything."

Harper looked perplexed. "Then why are you crying?"

"Because I fell in love with the stupid man. And now he's back at work and I'm here and, God, I'm such an idiot."

If Amy hadn't been so upset, she would have laughed at Harper's slack-jawed expression. "You fell in love? With my brother?"

Amy nodded.

Harper's shoulders drooped. "I'm so sorry, Amy. I should have warned you. It's just… I mean my brother may be a bit of a player, but he's never led a woman on or toyed with her emotions. I had no idea he would use you and then—"

"He didn't use me," Amy interrupted. "I think he might have fallen in love with me too." Neither of them had said the words, both cursed with too much self-preservation. She couldn't tell him how she felt knowing she had to leave and that nothing could come of her feelings. And besides, who the bloody hell fell in love with someone after only a week?

"Amy! You're home!"

Amy glanced behind Harper and saw Annie emerging from the big house. The sight of her friend caught her off-guard. *Annie did.* Her friend had fallen in love with Hunter Sullivan after a weeklong visit to Australia. In fact, she'd fallen so deeply for the boss at Farpoint, she'd uprooted her life in New York and moved halfway around the world to be with him.

Annie offered Amy a warm welcome-home hug. "We weren't expecting you until next weekend."

Amy shrugged, hoping her tears had dried enough to go unnoticed. "I got a little homesick." It was a lie and Annie was too shrewd to be fooled. Even so, she let it go.

"Hazel will be thrilled to see you. She's mentioned several times how much she's missed your spirit around this place."

Amy smiled, but didn't have a chance to respond.

Harper was still looking at her. In fact, her gaze hadn't moved since Amy had dropped her "love" bomb. "Andrew is in love with you?"

Amy lifted one shoulder. "I don't know that for sure. He never said he did. I just—"

"Of course he fell in love with you," Marc interjected. "I figure an American boy didn't stand a fighting chance against our Amy."

She laughed, the heaviness in her chest lifting. She was home, surrounded by people who loved her. She'd been right to cut the trip short and return. She needed their support, their strength to keep her going for the next few weeks…months.

Harper frowned. "But Andrew never—"

"He never falls in love," Amy finished. "Yeah. I know. Maybe it's wishful thinking on my part, but I'm okay with that. After all," her voice cracked slightly, "I'm most likely never going to see him again. It's just nice to believe my feelings were returned and it's not like it's going to hurt anyone for me to hold on to that idea."

Her hands trembled slightly, so she shoved them in the front pockets of her jeans.

"I hope you're right, Amy. I've always worried about

my brother's inability to let any woman into his heart. I should have known if anyone could do it, it would be you." Harper gave Amy another quick squeeze.

Annie reached for Amy's hand. "Come on into the house. You're going to have to tell Hazel and me all about this man."

Harper stepped over to say something to Keith and Amy wondered about Harper's sudden blush. It looked as if Harper and Keith had made their own love connection. Then Marc stepped closer and wrapped his arm around Harper in a way that seemed a touch more than friendly. Harper and Keith *and* Marc?

Harper gave her a shy shrug and Amy grinned. Her friend looked incredibly happy. Amy was relieved. She'd expected to find her friend still upset considering the sadness in Harper's voice the last time they'd spoken.

Annie grinned. "Those three have been inseparable since your friend arrived."

"Really?"

Annie winked at her then opened the front screen door. "I think I'll let Thomo and Blue fill you in on the details."

Keith took off his akubra, running his fingers through his sweat-matted hair, thanks to the hot day. It was a familiar gesture and just one more tiny insignificant thing that helped convince her she'd left heaven and landed smack-dab in the middle of reality.

This sucked.

"There's my girl." Hazel wiped her hands on her apron as she walked from the kitchen. Then she threw her arms out, capturing Amy in a tight squeeze. Hazel gave the best hugs on earth.

The tears Amy had just managed to stem began to flow once more, harder this time. Hazel's grip never slackened as Amy's cries turned to sobs.

"There, there, sweet lass. I'm sure it's not all as bad as that." Hazel continued to murmur soothing words while Amy cried out all the emotions she'd fought so hard to keep in for the past two days.

She led Amy to the couch where the two of them sat down. Annie claimed a nearby chair.

"I'm sorry." Amy reached for a tissue from the box on an end table, wiping her eyes and nose.

Hazel brushed Amy's hair away from her face. "It sounds like you've been holding those tears in for a while. What happened in Chicago, Amy?"

"I met a man."

Hazel glanced at Annie and rolled her eyes. "Dear God. What is it with you young people and these international romances?"

Amy laughed. Leave it to Hazel to find a way to ease the pain. "I didn't fall in love with him on purpose."

Annie leaned forward. "None of us ever do. The heart wants what the heart wants and practical things like jobs and geography rarely win out."

"So who is this man?" Hazel asked.

"Harper's brother, Andrew." Amy's throat squeezed when she spoke his name and she fought down a fresh round of tears. She was a mess.

Hazel pressed back against the cushions and studied Amy's face. "This is the man with the cable show, right? The one who lives your dream job, traveling all over the world?"

Amy nodded. She'd often related to Hazel the stories Harper had told her about Andrew's adventures. Many times, the two of them would pop online to look up the latest place he'd been just to see pictures and clips of the program. While Hazel had rarely left Farpoint—and never expressed the slightest bit of interest in seeing the world—

Amy suspected there was a tiny kernel of wanderlust in her boss as well.

"Well, that makes things interesting. I assume he's out jet-setting again?"

"He was in Chicago while I was there. We spent the week together and it was—"

"Magical." Annie supplied the word and Amy knew it was one she'd used to describe her first week on Farpoint with Hunter.

"Exactly." Amy didn't bother to deny it. "And stupid. I should never have let things go so far. I knew how they were going to end."

Hazel took her hands, tugging until Amy faced her more fully. "You didn't do a bloody thing wrong. Your willingness to open yourself up to life, to even risk heartbreak, is one of the things I admire about you, Amy. Ask yourself this. If you had it all to do over again, knowing what you know now, would you do it?"

"Hell yeah." Amy didn't even need to think about the response.

"Then it wasn't wrong, Amelia Wesson. You'll take some time, lick your wounds and you'll find a way to move on because you're smart, strong and brave."

A tear escaped before Amy could hold it back. She blinked rapidly, letting Hazel's words soothe her.

"I'm smart, strong and brave." Amy repeated the words, hoping that by speaking them aloud, they would take root.

"Just keep saying that."

"And if you want to fall apart or need a friendly ear, we'll be right here," Annie offered.

Amy smiled through her tears, grateful for her friends. No, the Sullivans had become family to her somewhere over the years. And despite that, she couldn't shake the emptiness looming inside her.

Smart, strong, brave. She wanted to believe that, but one word rang out louder.

Alone.

* * *

ANDREW STEPPED out of the helicopter and took a deep breath. Yep. Australia still smelled like fucking Vicks Vapo-Rub. Funny thing was he didn't mind as much this time. It made him think of Amy.

He smiled. Amy. He was so close to her now. Finally.

He saw a dust cloud coming down the road, kicked up by a truck. Obviously his arrival hadn't gone unnoticed. Not that he'd expected it to. Sort of hard to sneak onto a ranch by way of helicopter.

He still couldn't quite believe he was here. He'd gone back to work four days ago, meeting with the producers of *Off the Beaten Path*. As his paradise isle was still recovering from the monsoon, they'd needed to come up with an alternate location to shoot next.

For two days, Andrew pushed hard for Australia, using every ounce of persuasion in his body. Then, just when it looked like he was going to lose, the show's executive producer, Georgia Drake, asked to speak to him privately. She'd tilted her head and asked him what the hell was in Australia.

Like a lovesick fool, he'd confessed. And, to his surprise, he'd discovered that his ball-busting producer was a hopeless romantic at heart. She'd gone to bat for him and now he was here—on the cable company's dime—facing an even harder battle.

The truck pulled up to the tarmac and two men

emerged. He recognized Amy's two best friends, Marc and Keith, as they walked toward him. She'd shown him pictures of the men one night over dinner, cracking him up with stories about their childhood pranks. He nodded when they came to a stop in front of him.

The taller of the two men spoke first. "I'm Keith Munroe and this is Marc Thompson."

Andrew stuck out his hand. "I'm Andrew Shaw. Harper's brother."

"Yeah. We kinda figured that," Marc said, accepting his handshake.

"I understand my sister has been visiting here."

Keith crossed his arms. "Listen. While we respect a guy looking out for his sister, Harper's a woman now and more than capable of taking care of herself."

Andrew was surprised by Keith's defense of Harper. His initial thought was that they were the first line in keeping him away from Amy. "I know Harper can take care of herself."

"Is that right?" Marc asked.

Andrew struggled to understand what the fuck was going on. The men appeared to be as protective of his sister as he was. He wasn't sure whether he should be grateful they'd looked after her or insulted that they seemed to consider him a threat.

"I didn't come for Harper." Andrew wasn't sure why he was explaining himself to these two jackaroos or stockmen or whatever the hell they were.

Keith's entire body relaxed and a grin emerged. "Then you must be here for our Amy."

Our Amy. Andrew sucked in a deep breath. "No," he wanted to say. Amy was his.

Or so he prayed.

Then an uncomfortable thought emerged. "I was. But

now I'm thinking I might like to know what the hell is going on between you two and my sister."

Marc's anger faded and he looked chagrined. The guilty look had Andrew's fists clenching again. He knew it!

"Listen, mate," Keith raised his hands in surrender. "Harper and Amy are back at the main house. Why don't we give you a lift and we can all have a nice long chat?"

"Or you could answer my question here."

Keith didn't seem offended by his demand. Andrew's respect for the man notched up, despite his suspicions. It was clear one of these men was interested in Harper in a more-than-friendly way. Which meant one of them had upset her enough to call Amy crying. Problem was, Andrew couldn't figure out which of them was the villain.

"You're definitely gonna want to kick our arses later. But I think you need to talk to Harper before we get down to the brawlin'."

Our arses? Andrew wasn't sure what to make of that.

The image of him and Tom making love to Amy at Velvet Chains drifted through his mind. Then he looked at Marc's and Keith's somewhat guilty expressions and imagined the same scenario with the cowboys and Harper.

He'd fucking kill them.

"Come on." Keith turned before he could reply and Marc grabbed the bag at Andrew's feet. "I know two women who are going to be over the moon to see you."

Andrew followed, trying to calm down. He'd gone from excited to arrive, to nervous about seeing Amy, to pissed as hell over whatever the fuck Harper had been up to. If he didn't find a way to rein all of that in, he was going to screw up everything.

Marc—and his luggage—sat in the back of the truck while Andrew claimed the passenger seat. None of them spoke on the short ride back to what Keith had called the "main house". As he rode, it sank in how different his and Amy's lives truly were. He'd been raised a city boy, but this vast wilderness had been Amy's childhood home.

The truck stopped in front of a large, well-kept house. Andrew stepped out just as Harper emerged, standing on the front porch.

"Andrew?" Harper sprinted toward him, leaping into his arms. He embraced her, so fucking relieved to find her not only healthy, but happier than he'd seen her in years.

"Damn, you're a sight for sore eyes." He kissed the top of her head. "Never again, Harper. I swear to God, I don't care if you travel to China, you tell me. I promise I'll give you your space, but you have to at least tell me where you are, keep in touch."

"I've missed you so much. I'm sorry for leaving the way I did. I just wasn't sure how—"

"How to break loose of your insanely overprotective brother. I get it. I'm sorry I made you feel like you had to go to such extremes."

Harper shook her head. "I'm just as much to blame as you. I guess we're long overdue for a heart to heart chat."

Andrew nodded. Opening up to Amy had made him realize how long he and Harper had swept the past under the carpet, ignoring the elephant in the room rather than facing it and moving on. "Yeah. We are." Andrew looked around, aware their conversation could be overheard by the other men.

Harper noticed his glance. "What do you say we table the conversation until we get home? Enjoy Australia together."

He pulled her close for another hug. "Deal. Now… about Marc and Keith. What the hell is—"

"Andrew?"

He stopped speaking as Amy's voice sounded from

behind him. He released Harper, trying to figure out why his arms had suddenly gone numb.

Turning, he faced her. He grinned, so fucking happy to see her again. She was even more beautiful then he remembered.

She returned his smile, but her eyebrows lifted in rebuke. "So Harper was right. You did travel halfway around the world to find her."

He shook his head. "No. I came for you."

Her smile faded and he thought she suddenly looked pale. He stepped closer, worried she was going to pass out.

"For me?" she whispered, tears forming in the corner of her eyes.

Had he misread everything last week? Been so blinded by his own feelings that he'd failed to realize they weren't returned?

An older woman cleared her throat loudly, distracting him.

"I think," she said, as everyone turned to face her, "that we should leave Amy and her gentleman alone. I'm Hazel Sullivan, by the way. Nice to meet you, Andrew."

He nodded by way of introduction, struggling to find his voice. Harper gave him an encouraging smile as she followed Keith and Marc into the house.

"You seriously flew all this way to see me?"

Amy's bewildered tone had him turning once more. "Of course, I did."

"What about your job?"

He lifted one shoulder. "I'm actually here under the guise of scoping out a new location. And to hire a personal assistant."

She frowned. "You want to do a story on Australia? Haven't you already done that?"

She'd missed the most important part. Even so, he

nodded. "My producer is in discussions with a nearby cattle station. One that's open to tourists. I think it's sort of the equivalent of a dude ranch back home."

She seemed to consider that. "Sounds cool."

"And do you think you might be persuaded to accept my job offer?"

Amy blinked rapidly. "What job offer?"

"I want you to work as my personal assistant, Amy. Part of my contract negotiations said that I could hire someone to help me prepare for my trips, to travel with me, to keep me on schedule."

Her mouth dropped open. "And you want me?"

"I've witnessed your researching abilities firsthand. I grew up in Chicago and you managed to show me things I'd never seen. And your itinerary was superior. I could really use someone with your skills out on the road."

His astute Amy didn't waste any time asking the hard question. "And just how *personally* would I be assisting you?"

He grinned ruefully. "That's up to you. I'm not going to lie. That one week wasn't enough for me. Maybe this isn't an ideal situation, the perfect way to pursue a relation-ship, but I don't have a fucking clue how else to do it. You live in Australia and I live in America. This was the only way I could figure out to get us in the same time zone. I want to date you, Amy. I want to see if what I think I'm feeling is real. I need to be with you to do that."

Amy took his hand and squeezed it. "I'd like to explore my feelings as well."

"Give me one year. Hit the road with the show for twelve months. If things go south and you decide you hate me, you can come home. And, in the meantime, you'll have marked some of those dream places off your travel list."

Amy nodded slowly. "It sounds so tempting, but there are so many things that would have to be worked out."

"I know I'm asking you to give up a lot. I mean I'd be asking you to leave your home, your job."

Amy's face brightened. "My job." Her smile grew. "Don't worry about that. I think I know a suitable replacement for Farpoint's schoolteacher."

Andrew's gaze narrowed. "Shit. You're thinking of Harper, aren't you?"

She shrugged. "Maybe. Maybe not."

"What the hell is going on between my sister and those cowboys?"

"They're not cowboys, Andrew."

"Damn it, Amy. I'm not playing semantics with you."

"Let's just say that you owe my friends a favor. While you were being nice to me in Chicago, they were being very nice to your sister here."

He swallowed heavily, beating back the sudden rush of anger.

"And before you go into that house with guns blazing, I think you need to talk to Harper about it. And maybe you could try *really* listening to her. You know, pay attention."

He chuckled. Saucy little wench. God, he loved her.

His breath caught, then he threw caution and common sense to the wind. "I love you, Amy."

She wrapped her arms around his waist, looking up into his face, her eyes shining with happy tears. "I love you, too."

Epilogue

Amy shielded her eyes with her hand as she looked out over the expanse of valley below. Andrew spoke to the camera. They were in Virginia this week and had just tackled Blackrock. The lush, green valley was more beautiful in real life than the pictures she'd studied online and trillium was blooming all around them.

She glanced at Andrew's handsome face and smiled. They'd had so many adventures together this year. He filled her days with discovery and her nights with passion.

"Hey, Amy. The rest of the crew is about to head back down before it gets dark. Last chance to change your mind and sleep in the comfort of the hotel. Tom says it gets cold up here in April."

She knew he was teasing her, trying to get her to give in. They'd sort of dared each other to do some back-country camping while on this excursion. There was a definite chill in the air that they wouldn't be able to counteract with a campfire. Fires weren't allowed.

Even so, she wasn't worried about the cold.

"I'll be fine. But if you're backing out—"

Tom laughed and gestured for the rest of the crew to pick up their equipment. "These two will never cry uncle. Let's roll. See you guys tomorrow afternoon. Happy anniversary."

Amy grinned. It had been one year to the day since she'd agreed to join Andrew as his personal assistant. Obviously, Andrew had told his best friend they were celebrating. They'd agreed to talk tonight about her job and the relationship. Amy jokingly referred to it as their contract renewal negotiations.

Andrew didn't speak as the others left. Instead, he took her hand and the two of them picked their way through the woods, following the path to the camp they'd set up earlier in the day.

When they arrived, Andrew unzipped the tent and gestured for her to crawl inside. The wind was picking up and their chilly night was indeed turning cold. They would have to eat their simple dinner inside, sheltered from the brisk air.

As soon as they were snug in the tight space, Andrew sank down, pulling her with him to cuddle on his sleeping bag. She relished the familiarity of his arms. They'd spent month after month in each other's arms. Amy had never regretted her decision to leave home, to follow her heart.

"Happy anniversary." He'd mentioned the one-year milestone a few times today and she sensed he was anxious to see if she would return home or stay.

Foolish man. Was it really a question?

Sitting up, she reached for the tiny flask she'd snuck into her backpack. Uncapping it, she lifted it. "Here's to many, many more years."

She took a sip then passed the Bundy to him. She'd made a rum lover of him this past year.

He accepted the flask then added to her toast. "Here's

to a lifetime." Rather than take a drink, he reached into his pocket.

Amy's heart began to race the moment he pulled out the small ring box.

Andrew flipped the lid back, revealing the most beautiful engagement ring she'd ever seen. "Marry me, Amy."

So much for popping the question. Andrew, in typical fashion, made it a demand.

And as always, she responded in kind. "Hurry up and put that ring on my finger."

They laughed as he slid the diamond in place.

The perfect fit.

WANT *to learn how Harper finds her happy ending? Check out* Sharing Their Lover, *then read the rest of the Crossed Wires stories! The entire series is available now!*

Taming His Princess
Claiming Her Cowboy
Finding Her Master
Sharing Their Lover

If you enjoyed this story, please consider leaving a review.

About the Author

Virginia native Mari Carr is a New York Times and USA TODAY bestseller of contemporary erotic romance novels. With over one million copies of her books sold, Mari was the winner of the Romance Writers of America's Passionate Plume award for her novella, Erotic Research. She has over a hundred published works, including her popular Wild Irish and Compass books, along with the Trinity Masters series she writes with Lila Dubois.

Subscribe to Mari's Newsletter

Lexxie Couper started writing when she was six and hasn't stopped since. She's not a deviant, but she does have a deviant's imagination and a desire to entertain readers with her words. Add the two together and you get romances that can make you laugh, cry, shake with fear or tremble with desire. Sometimes all at once. When she's not submerged in the worlds she creates, Lexxie's life revolves around her family, a husband who thinks she's insane, an indoor cat who likes to stalk shadows, and her daughters, who both utterly captured her heart and changed her life forever.

Contact Lexxie at lexxie@lexxiecouper.com, follow her on Twitter twitter.com/lexxie_couper or visit her at www.lexxiecouper.com where she occasionally makes a fool of herself on her blog.